DADDY'S
Girl

DADDY'S

Girl

ISABELLA STARLING
DEMI DONOVAN

Contents

CHAPTER 1

Law

$\mathcal{S}$ HE WAS MADE TO SUCK my cock. She just didn't know it yet.

The moment I saw her, my hand reached into my jacket pocket, pulling out the tattered cigarettes. When I touched one to my lips, it would have only been fair if it had burst into flame without any heat.

The concrete cool against my shoulder, I took the first drag, my eyes never leaving her as she bounded down to the platform, lugging a suitcase almost as big as she was behind her.

I would have recognized her anywhere. Her image was

ingrained in my brain, like a vision I couldn't shake. The pictures didn't do her any justice. I knew they wouldn't.

She was mine. I knew it as clearly as I knew that she would be twisted around my cock in a few days, begging for more through tears of pain and lust.

The smoke filled my lungs and then plumed out, billowing in front of me in the shadow of the train station. She couldn't see me, but I could see her as clear as day. Even with people standing and moving in front of her, it was like I could see right through them. They couldn't hide her from me.

Nothing could. It was too late to run, too late to hide.

Those long, pale legs, carelessly shown off in floral shorts, would look so much better with red welts running across them. That plump ass of hers would be so much riper with whip marks all over it. Her whole body needed to be taught, trained, shown what it was made for.

To serve, to please, to be used.

And those gorgeous, full pink lips were only made for begging. I could hear her voice in my head, calling for me, pleading with me, and I hadn't even heard her speak yet. I just knew. Like I knew everything about her, everything she needed and everything she wanted.

Everything she was going to get.

She was smiling, but her expression was strained as she hugged a woman years her senior. Her blonde hair was tied back in a ponytail and her low-cut top was showing everyone too much. I had to fight the urge to go to her and throw my leather jacket over her shoulders, cover her up from the leering gazes.

She wasn't for anyone else's eyes, just mine. In all her innocence and in all her shamelessness, she was mine and mine alone and she needed to learn that.

The smoke felt heavy on my lips, and I exhaled roughly, tersely. She was moving away now, her face turned away from me.

I knew I would enjoy yanking that pretty little chin of hers up toward me soon, making her look at me with those big blue eyes even if she didn't want to meet my gaze. I would show her what it felt like to get all the attention she was begging for, and what the price of it really was. What happened to little girls who didn't know how to behave.

How she had made it so long without coming across another man like me, I would never know. I didn't care to think about it, either.

It could have been so much worse, babygirl, I thought, an unpleasant memory somewhere just on the edges of my consciousness.

She was mine now. Making it so was just a formality. Everyone, and everything else, was unimportant.

With her ponytail bobbing in the crowd, disappearing from sight, I took the last drag of the cigarette and threw it on the ground, stepping on it with a booted foot. Shoving my hands in my pockets, I pushed myself away from the building and slowly walked after her and her companion, too far to really see her anymore, but walking right in her path.

I could smell her in the air. Even in a train station with thousands of people milling through it every day, it was like I could sense her clearly, track her without fail. That's how it is with your property.

You can always find that which is yours.

"Excuse me," someone chirped, distracting me.

I stopped, frowning as my gaze fell on a redhead that any other day would have had my attention. She was everything I liked. Young. Innocent. Needing to be taught some manners.

Her pink tongue slicked over her red lips as she batted her lashes at me. There was too much make-up on her face. It made her look older than the barely eighteen she must have been. Her friend covered her mouth and giggled as they shared a quick look among one another.

I didn't have to ask what she wanted. It was painted all over her face. Whether she was going to disguise it behind asking for a smoke or for directions or for some other bullshit, it didn't matter. She couldn't lie to me as well as she could to herself.

I had to wonder how long she'd been psyching herself up for this. I had to wonder if she knew what kind of danger she'd put herself in. Not only by approaching a wolf, but one who was after something much more valuable than she could ever be. She could be eaten alive, and not in the way she was begging to.

I turned away from her, not bothering with a reply, instinctively looking for my babygirl in the direction she'd been walking in. Red grabbed my sleeve, yanking me toward herself with brazenness far beyond her years.

"Careful, little girl," I growled, my gray eyes flashing.

She practically jumped away from me. Her friend took two steps back, the innocence and youth of their years now finally showing on their faces. Both were dressed too revealing. Both were too dumb to be let out alone.

With a growl in the back of my throat, I grabbed Red by the arm and pulled her up to me. The excitement burning in her eyes, the way her chest rose and fell in her barely-there top, it would have made my blood burn any other time. Right now, though, she was just a fucking annoyance.

"You shouldn't try and play with men who are old enough to be your daddy, little girl," I snarled at her.

The little sigh she let slip out between her lips was almost inviting. For a moment, I saw my babygirl in her, like someone had superimposed an image of her over this teenager desperate to be destroyed by a force she didn't understand. It was gone as soon as it hit me.

Red wasn't good enough to lick her boots.

"Is that what you want? For me to call you daddy?" Red asked, jutting her chin out and trying to stand tall.

I grinned.

She was going to get herself into the worst kind of trouble. It just wasn't going to be with me.

"Be careful with what you wish for," I said, releasing her.

Instead of stepping away, she nearly toppled into me, wanting to lean into me so badly.

I could easily see myself taking her home. Tying her tan wrists, pulling her up by them and leaving her there until she learned some manners. Keeping her in place until she begged and screamed and wailed for me, telling me she'd never be bad again, that she'd never be a fucking brat again. Torturing her by not giving her what she needed until she was a step from losing her mind, and then breaking her until she was nothing but a shattered pile of desperation.

But she was too late. I was off the market. I didn't have time for trash, time for distraction.

"Wait," she squeaked, the familiar rosy pink blush of lust tinting her cheeks as I left her behind me.

I didn't look back, just kept walking. Blood surged in my veins. I couldn't afford any distractions today, not when I was so close.

I reached for another cigarette, lighting it as I walked and taking a long, irritated drag from it.

Now that she was so close, every second away from her was too long. I had to have her.

Right fucking now.

CHAPTER 2

Lily

"Y ou've been staring at him all night, Lily," Alexandra said, nudging my side with her bony hip. I gave her a mean look and she reciprocated with an eye-roll.

"You should go over there." She grinned like a Cheshire cat. She was so annoying. "Some other girl might snatch him up any minute."

I saw the way Alexandra eyed him, her chocolate-brown eyes seizing the man in question. She wanted him, too, and it was exactly the push I needed to gain some confidence.

"Saw him first," I said in my sweetest voice. Flashing Alexandra a smile that said fuck you, I turned on my heel and strode toward the bar. I risked a look over my shoulder, just in time to see her sulky expression before she turned her back on me.

I smirked to myself, and then looked back ahead, focusing on the task at hand.

I kept my eyes focused on him as I walked over. He was the epitome of tall, dark and handsome. The glass tumbler he held in his hand looked tiny in his grip, like he could shatter it with a simple squeeze. He had dark hair; so deep brown it was almost black. Gray eyes, stormy, and surprisingly light compared to his other features.

He was also much, much older than me. I'd gotten in with my fake ID just fine—I looked older than I was anyway. No one in here probably knew I was eighteen, my makeup took care of it just fine, and mommy's money paid for the best fake ID money could buy.

But this man, he must've been in his late thirties, maybe even early forties. He was gorgeous, almost making me blush by taking a single look at him. Much, much too old for me.

He wasn't just handsome. He was the kind of guy who you'd want to get in trouble for... A guy I'd beg to spank me, and show me just how bad I'd been.

Subconsciously, I bit my bottom lip. I had a feeling Mr. Mysterious played rough. Maybe he'd be the one rough enough to hurt me.

His eyes found mine, and a fire burned me from the inside. His gaze held dark promises. Ones I hoped he would keep.

I strolled up to the bar and stood next to him, all dolled up in my six-inch heels and a too-short dress that showed off my best assets.

"Hi," I said softly, giving him a shy smile.

He looked unimpressed as he raised the glass to his lips, taking a long, deep sip. He was absolutely delicious, even better up close. I felt myself smiling like a cat, knowing I could be under him with a wink and a lewd gesture. Fuck, I wanted it.

"Hello, trouble," he responded in a low growl. His voice made me yearn for more words. Filthy words. It also made me want to beg for the feel of his palm slapping my ass. Fuck, I was already in too deep.

"Want to get me a drink?" I asked the stranger sweetly, fluttering my lashes like a doll. My heart was beating too fast though, threatening to rip apart my chest. I felt like I'd collapse at his feet at any moment.

His pause was too long, and I took the time to look him over again. He was good-looking, but with an edge.

The kind of man you couldn't trust not to fuck you over. Despite his expensive clothes, he looked like he knew the bar well. And that was strange, since it was a seedy place downtown. My mom would kill me, knowing I'd let my friends drag me along.

The stranger looked at me hard, his strange gray eyes boring into me. "No," he said simply. "I want to bend you over my knee and teach you some manners."

I blushed, deep crimson blooming over my cheeks. He had a mouth on him... a mouth I hoped he knew how to use. I was already getting wet, the seedy club where no one recognized me only making me hornier. The dirtier, the better.

"You don't think I'm a good girl?" I asked daringly, stepping closer. A scent of leather and whiskey enveloped me. Coupled with his musk, it was a heady, lusty fragrance. One I wanted to taste. He was dark, dangerous. Rich, by the looks of that leather jacket and the Italian shoes he was wearing.

I looked right into those gray eyes, so light they almost looked wrong in that handsome, chiseled face. His skin was smooth and devoid of wrinkles, but his eyes spoke about his age.

"What makes you think I don't donate millions to charity, and spend my spare time playing with stray puppies?"

"I can smell the money on you from a mile away," he smirked at me, giving me a look that made me feel dirty, even though I'd taken a milk bath before coming to the club.

My smile faltered, only for a split second. Long enough for him to see, though.

"And you're a bad actress. I don't buy the rich bitch act for a second."

His gaze was hard, patronizing. I hated it, but not as much as I loved it. I wanted him to humiliate me. I yearned for more dirty words coming from his mouth, calling me names, forcing me to my knees.

"Do you even know who I am?" I asked, my voice shakier than I would've liked it to be. The words were on the tip of my tongue. Lily Kingsley. My mom owns this town, you motherfucker. "I'm-"

"Do I look like a give a fuck who you are?" he interrupted. I looked around, feeling a bit unsure of myself. He was mean. A real prick.

He smirked at me. Then he leaned in closer, his lips brushing my ear in a way that made me shiver. His thick fingers pushed my long blonde hair aside, the silky strands falling down my back. I gasped as he grabbed my chin, pulling me closer, his lips brushing my sensitive skin.

"Still, I think your mouth can take a big cock," he said,

tugging on my hair ever so slightly. Just enough to make me gasp out loud. "I want to see you gagging on my dick. How about it, Barbie doll?"

He moved away again, giving me an expectant look. I was left gaping at him, unsure of whether I'd just imagined the whole thing.

"You... what?" I babbled, but he didn't grace me with another look. Instead, he emptied his glass and set it down on the bar with a thud. The music was loud, but I was too lost in our encounter to notice the drop of the bass.

He got up from the barstool, and I watched, mesmerized, as he threw a hundred-dollar bill on the counter. Approaching me again, he took hold of my hair and pulled my head back, hard.

My whole body flushed, deep red stains on my neck and my chest. His beautiful eyes evaluated me like I was a piece of meat, ready for his hungry mouth to devour.

I wanted him to bite me.

"This way, babygirl," the stranger ordered, pulling on my hair until I followed him obediently. I didn't dare look for my friends; instead following mystery man toward the door marked 'exit'.

I stumbled in my heels once we reached the alley, the smell of sweat from the club being replaced by fresh, cold air. It was followed by the sensation of his warm hand on my arm, gripping me hard. I looked up into those light eyes, and I felt scared.

I also felt a rush of excitement, so intense it made my skin prickle.

"Bend over," he growled, barely parting his lips to get the words out. The back door of the club shut behind us with a loud clang and I swallowed the lump in my throat.

His other hand went up to my throat, gripping it lightly between his fingers. "You heard me, rich girl. Bend over... right the fuck now."

I did as I was told, my hands braced against the wall as he moved behind me. His hands found my ass and I gasped as he pushed my dress up.

This wasn't a good time to tell him I'd never done this. Never had a man inside me, not even someone's fingers. I would keep it to myself, I decided.

"That's a good girl," he said through gritted teeth, his palm cupping my ass and slapping it lightly. "Fuck, so tight."

I was more turned on than ever. It was so wrong, so dirty. My mom would kill me if she knew what I was doing. But it felt so good to feel the stranger's hands on me. It felt good to hear the dirty words rolling off his tongue.

He pushed my thong aside and I gasped out loud. He was so fast, so full of intent. He didn't give me a second to consider what was happening. He stroked his thumb up my pussy lips and I let out a moan. I loved it, and it gave me a rush that almost knocked me over.

His fingers held my ass firmly, and he spread me wide open. I heard him growl deep in his throat, and I knew I was dripping wet. I could feel his hungry eyes on my snatch, and I wanted to feel him inside me.

"Tell me you want me to fuck your cunt," he growled, and I moaned aloud, but no words would make it from my lips. I could feel him growing impatient, his grip tightening on my ass. Finally, he grabbed my shoulders and pulled me closer, making me face him. His handsome face was twisted in an expression of rage.

"I said, tell me," he said, and I cowered under his touch.

"I... I can't," I said softly, embarrassed of my own weakness.

His grip tightened once more. "Say it," he demanded.

All I could do was shake my head regretfully. I couldn't speak to him like that. I loved dirty talk, but I never reciprocated. Maybe I was too shy, or just too uptight, to play a dirty girl.

He leaned over, his lips gently brushing my cheek and I gasped out loud again. "Please," I begged softly. "Please, just..."

"Just what?" he demanded, his fingers trailing down my arm, his lips dangerously close to mine. God, I could feel my nipples tighten beneath my dress, I wanted him so badly, his searing kiss on my needy lips. My mouth had already parted in expectation of his lips on mine, yet the kiss didn't come. He was teasing me, and I loved it. I loved playing games.

"Just kiss me," I begged, my breaths now heavy.

"And?" He was relentless, and I realized he wasn't going to give up unless I gave him what I wanted.

"Fuck me, please," I begged, desperate for him to turn me around again, yearning for his thick fingers rubbing my slit. He didn't do what I asked, though, instead claiming my mouth with his. Just as good, if not better.

He was demanding, biting and licking me until I was gasping for breath, moaning for him to keep going. Our lips were bound together in a vicious act of passion, and I felt the chilly air against the wetness marking my legs.

I grabbed his hand and pushed it between my legs. I placed his thick fingers against my entrance, gently trying to make him touch me. He wouldn't oblige, but his meaty finger slid across my clit and I moaned.

"Fuck," I yelped, the sensation almost too much, but so damn good nonetheless. I eased into his hand, moving along with him as he teased me to an orgasm. He was still kissing me, hungry and desperate for the wet feel of my tongue.

He slapped my thighs apart and I moaned again, needing him so badly. All the while, alarms were going off in my mind and I knew just how wrong it all was. Yet I couldn't stop... the dirty feeling only made it that much better.

"Keep them spread," he said into my ear, his voice raspy, and he guided my legs apart as I begged him to keep touching, working my clit. His fingers were dipping in and out, skilled to perfection. I knew I was about to come, so close to the edge I could smell the sweet scent of my orgasm already.

"Good girl," the stranger murmured again, and he took my wrists in his free hand, twisting them behind my back. I gasped at the pain in my bones, now desperate to come. He obliged, twisting them into an uncomfortable position behind me. I thrashed under him.

"Fuck, stay still." It wasn't a request.

He held me in place and pinched my clit so hard I cried and came, cursing out loud as my pussy squelched and he picked up speed. I shuddered and bucked and jerked on his hand. A long stream of dirty words fell from my mouth and I trembled in his arms, shaken by the intensity of my orgasm. I felt him move away, his fingers leaving my throbbing clit alone.

And then he picked me up like I weighed nothing, taking me in his arms. I snuggled close to him, needing more of him. I wanted to taste every inch of his skin, have him drag his tongue over mine and feel me shake under it. I wanted him to show me all the rules we could break together. I wanted to be fucked...

My eyes were filled with lust as he threw me over his shoulder and gripped me tightly around my thighs.

Stupid fucking instincts. Fooled by his handsome face, misguided by the hot and heavy way he'd made me come. I never even fought him, not when he carried me over to the car, not even when he pushed me inside.

"Where are we going?" I purred, tired, but content. I was ready for round two, and I hoped he was taking me to a nice swanky hotel. I couldn't wait to ruin their sheets.

He didn't answer, his mouth set in a thin line as he placed me on the backseat. He wouldn't look at my eyes, and I think that was when I really started to get scared. I didn't even know his name. I wanted to ask what he was doing, but I didn't even know what to call him. Such a filthy girl, sleeping with a nameless stranger.

"Sorry, babygirl," he smirked at me. He was standing outside the car, his huge figure looming over me.

He finally looked at me, his expression hard and

unrelenting as he reached for me. He pulled on my hair again, making my head drop back and a hot breath escape my lips. And then something covered my mouth, a rancid smell entering through my nostrils and making me gag.

I tried to move away, but it was too late. I was already drifting, gauzy fingers of unconsciousness wrapping around my mind.

CHAPTER 3

Law

I COULD KEEP WATCHING HER FOREVER.

I still couldn't believe she was here, right in front of me. My Lily.

So fucking pure, so fucking innocent, even if she tried to hide under that façade of a brat. I knew that wasn't her. Not entirely, anyway. She just needed to be reminded of it.

My fingers drummed against the concrete wall in the dark room, illuminated by a single bulb in the ceiling. There were no windows and aside from the bathroom a door away, the chair Lily was tied to and a mattress on the floor, there were no furnishings. Just gray walls and my babygirl, lighting the place up.

I must have been standing there for hours, just watching her, waiting for her to wake up. She'd been so fucking dirty in the bar, my hands itched to teach her a lesson, but I couldn't bring myself to wake her up. She begged for this, coming to me like a moth to a flame. It was way too fucking easy.

Running my hand through my dark hair, I felt my insides twist. My cock had been rock hard since she approached me and I couldn't stop picturing her lips around it, sucking me off with tears running down her pretty face.

The waiting was killing me, far more than when I didn't have her yet. Then, it had felt like penance, something I had to go through to deserve her. But now she was here and I was running out of patience.

Grabbing the pail of cold water that was sitting on the floor next to the door, I splashed half of it in her face. She sputtered and screeched as I set it down again, crossing my arms over my chest then. I stood tall in front of her, towering above her with the cramped room barely large enough for me to avoid crouching.

Her mascara dribbled down her cheeks slightly, leaving

dark lines as she squeezed her eyes shut and then fluttered them open.

"What the fuck," she hissed, looking at me with shock and disgust and fear.

It was the latter I liked the most. The disgust? Well, she hadn't seen anything yet.

"Morning, princess," I said with a smirk, reaching forward to tuck a strand of wet blonde hair out of her face.

For a moment, she stood perfectly still, maybe even moved forward slightly. Then, as if realizing what she was doing, she recoiled as if slapped in the face. I gritted my teeth, annoyed.

"Don't fucking touch me," she screeched, and there was a note of hysteria in it now.

I chuckled, smoothing her hair back anyway. Then, before she could whine again, I grabbed her chin and yanked upward, making her look me in the eye. Her face was so fucking close to my cock, it was torture not to give her what she so clearly needed—me. But I had to be patient.

"You don't get to make the rules anymore, babygirl," I told her, my voice low and level. "If you're good, I might allow you to make a decision again one day, but that day isn't now. You're *mine* and you need to understand that this means you need to be a good girl for me. You want to be a good girl for me, don't you, *Lily*?" There was no hint of a smile on my face anymore. She just stared at me, dumb-struck, those sweet lips of her parted and her expression blank. It must have finally been sinking in that she wasn't in fucking Kansas anymore, and puppies and rainbows wouldn't get her out of the mess she was in.

"Don't you?" I asked again, growling it this time as I squeezed her cheeks between my fingers.

Her skin was so soft to the touch.

"No," she said suddenly, sitting up a little straighter in the chair she was restrained to.

I moved my head out of the way when she tried to spit at me, the spittle smearing across my black shirt. I couldn't help but grin. She was everything I had expected her to be, and more.

Without a word, I smacked her across the face, her head flying to the side. She let out a wince, a sound that echoed through me and seemed to fill me up to the core. She sounded so good when she hurt.

Looking up at me, her blue eyes filled with hurt, I could tell that no one had probably called her on her bull-shit in a long, long time. I put my hand on the red of her cheek, her flesh hot against my cool palm. She shied away from it, but she had nowhere to go.

"Do you want to try that again?" I asked.

She didn't have a response this time.

"That's what I thought," I said, grinning.

She would learn, but a part of me hoped that she wouldn't do it too fast. I had too much to show her, and I had been waiting for too long to make it go fast. My cock twitched in my jeans as I drank in the sight of her quivering before me, goosebumps running up her bare arms now, and those streaks of mascara hiding tears she probably wanted to cry.

Reluctantly, I took my hand from her cheek and turned my back on her for a moment, grabbing a smoothie from the floor. I wasn't going to untie her yet, but she'd been out like a light for hours now. It was practically noon. She needed to keep her energy up for everything that I had planned for the two of us.

"Please. Just let me go, no one has to know this happened," she said as I carried the smoothie to her, bringing the straw to her lips. "I've got money. Whatever you want, you can have it."

"Drink," I told her, ignoring her babbling.

I knew exactly what she had, how much or how little. Money wasn't what I wanted, and I was sure she knew that. She wasn't that fucking dumb.

She resisted for a moment, eyeing the pinkish drink dubiously, the drops of cold water still beading on her skin. Then, with one quick glance at me to confirm that I meant what I said, she took a tentative sip. After that, she drank almost the entire thing.

No one could say I wasn't an *attentive* monster, at least.

"Good girl," I murmured when she was done, and she gave me the slightest smile.

Just like the pictures, she was perfect. Even better than what I'd seen and imagined. Filth on something so clean usually did that.

"You're going to let me go, right?" she asked, that voice of hers shaking harder than the rest of her was.

I set the plastic cup and straw down by her chair and cocked a brow at her. At 6'6", I would have dwarfed her even if she weren't tied to a chair, but I must have looked like a giant to her then. Dressed in black, stubble on my chin, muscles cording, I bet I was her worst nightmare, and her sweetest daydream all rolled into one.

"Now why would I do that?" I asked her conversationally.

"But-" she started, stuttering as her brow furrowed. "I..."

"You what, Lily?" I asked.

I think she only now realized that I had called her by her name.

"What do you want from me?" she asked, swallowing hard.

I didn't need to think about that.

"Everything," I told her.

She gaped at me and it made me think back to how she'd been at the club. Begging for me to fuck her, at the same time incapable of getting the words out of her mouth. I had to resist the urge to bring my fingers to my lips, to taste the ghost of sweetness that my mind convinced me lingered on them. I hadn't even penetrated her but her pussy was so fucking inviting to me.

The way she moaned and screamed when she came, the way she obviously wanted more, wanted to be twisted around my cock like the good little slut that she was... It was enough to drive a man insane.

"Do you remember how you begged at the bar?" I asked, my fingers tightening on my arm. "Do you remember how you asked me to fuck you? How you came, screaming like a whore in a back alley? Do you remember that, babygirl?"

She closed her mouth, lashes fluttering as she looked down at her lap. Her cheeks were now red, both of them, embarrassment creeping up in her. Such a fucking brat, yet she still had the decency to be ashamed of how needy she was for cock. Like a good girl.

I grabbed her by the hair and yanked her head back, making her scream. She should have learned by now that when I asked a question, I wanted a fucking answer.

"You're hurting me!"

"You don't know what pain is, sweetheart," I seethed, not letting her go. "I asked you a question."

With her bottom lip quivering, I saw a spark come to life in her eyes. Rebellion, spite. My bratty little monster. I had to bite down on the inside of my mouth to hide my smile.

"Yes," she said finally. "I remember."

"Are you ashamed of being a whore?"

"You can't talk to me like that," she gasped, eyes wide.

When I pulled back on her hair again, she whimpered. Her legs were tied to the chair, but I shoved her knees apart and reached down, shoving my hand between her thighs. I felt her clench up but she couldn't keep me from ripping her wet, pink thong aside and pushing my hand against her slit.

She was soaking wet. I could have shoved three fingers in her right then, if I wanted to. And it took more than I would have liked to admit to keep from doing that.

I contained myself, just running my thumb over her clit a few times, hard. She twitched, her body rigid, as I kept her head back and her pale neck exposed. Without thinking about it, I leaned in and kissed her swan neck, the first touch gentle.

It didn't last long.

I rubbed her pussy harder, my fingers aching to dig into her as I sucked on her neck, leaving teeth marks and bruises.

She whimpered, but the sounds turned into needy moans, pleasure and pain rolled into one just the way I liked it. Just like I knew she needed it.

"Yes," she finally breathed, breathless. "Yes, I remember!"

It was like I was kicked out of a trance. My eyes flew open and I flicked my thumb across her clit one more time, rubbed my thick fingers against her slit so hard that I was almost pushing into her, but not quite. I knew she couldn't be far from coming, the glazed over look in her eyes telling me everything I needed to know.

Mine. All mine.

And no one could ever take her away from me again.

She was breathing heavy as I let go of her hair. Making sure she was watching me, I brought my hand to my mouth and slowly licked across my fingers, keeping eye contact with her. My fingers glistened with her juices, her sweet, virgin pussy the best aphrodisiac.

I didn't need to fuck her to know she's never been touched. She might have been trying to hide it from me, but I knew she'd never been split open by a cock before.

I was going to enjoy every second of it when it finally fucking happened.

She moaned as my tongue slipped out and I smirked once I was done cleaning her off my fingers. Next time, I would let her do it, but she needed to learn some manners before that.

I could see the question in her eyes.

Why hadn't I finished her off?

Why hadn't I let her come, let her scream again?

Because I shouldn't have done it the first time.

I couldn't reward her for being a bad girl when she needed to be good for me. My little girl needed to be perfect, and then she could have whatever she fucking wanted.

"Better," I told her, admiring the bruises already forming on her neck, the red glow of her cheeks, the mascara running down her cheeks. "If you're a good girl, I can make you feel good again. But bad girls... Well, do you know what happens to bad girls?"

She squared her jaw, trying to look like the haughty rich bitch that she still thought she was. She didn't know yet that she would never be one again.

"They get punished?" she asked me, sarcasm dripping from her words even though I knew she was soaking wet for me, her pink pussy still throbbing for my touch.

I grinned.

"Exactly."

That's when I turned to leave, taking the key from my pocket and unlocking the door. The moment the click of the lock sounded, I heard her stir.

"Wait," Lily gasped. "You can't leave me down here alone! I... I don't even know your name! Just... just call my mom, she'll give you whatever you want for me! I can give you her number, it's-"

"No one's coming for you, babygirl," I told her with a shake of my head, the thought filling me with warmth. "It's just you and me now."

I considered leaving her there on the chair, but I was not sure when I would be able to come back. Reluctantly, I slipped behind her and cut the ties on one of her hands. She went rigid when she felt the blade too close to her skin.

I didn't bother with the rest of the binds, but I crouched down and clicked a metal cuff around her ankle. I was sure she would have wriggled herself out of the rest of the binds by the time I was back, but she couldn't get out of this.

I didn't look at her as I got up and exited out through the door. But I couldn't deny her too much.

She'd been so good, and quiet, her ragged breathing

the only thing telling me that her heart was beating out of her chest. Before I could tell myself that she didn't deserve to know yet, I told her what she wanted to know.

"Lawson," I said, revealing my name.

Then the door fell shut and I locked it, heading up the stairs and out of the cellar, taking two steps at a time.

I needed to get away from her fast, or I might have just gone back and never left.

I stepped out of the cellar and into a brightly lit, carefully decorated hallway. There was barely anything on the walls, other than a few nondescript paintings that probably cost a fortune. There was a white carpet underneath my shoes and I tracked dark shoeprints as I stalked across it. The corridor itself was three times the size that Lily's cell was, and the house was a fucking mansion in its own right.

"Lawson, is that you?" Emily yelled from the dining room.

I grunted a nondescript response at her. I couldn't deal with her sneering face right now. I walked past the dining room and headed toward my study, but before I could disappear into it, she popped out behind me.

Long, carefully coiffed blonde hair framing her face, she was a picture of old wealth with those high cheekbones and her white Chanel cocktail dress.

I couldn't even look her in the eye.

"Is she settling in alright?" she asked me with a casual smile, like we were talking about a new pet puppy.

"She'll be fine," I told her, cutting the conversation short.

"Don't forget that we need to plan that luncheon," she yelled after me with a bored tone as I closed the door to my study, every muscle in my body rigid with irritation.

It was only when my gaze met the wall across from my wide, mahogany desk that I could catch my breath and calm down. The walls were covered with pictures of Lily.

I could barely believe I finally had the real thing.

And she was all mine.

CHAPTER 4

Lily

I HATED IT WHEN HE WAS around, but I almost hated it more when he left me to myself like this. Rage bubbled right under my surface, threatening to spill over like hot molten lava. The worst part was being alone, sending shivers down my spine and making me panic, thinking he would never come back.

But being left alone with my thoughts was horrible too, wondering and killing myself over the image of Law with some other woman. I didn't know where he went off to when he left, but I had this feeling he had someone else, someone who didn't know about me and someone who shared his bed during the night. I hated her already, my body burning up with anger whenever I thought about the mysterious woman.

I'd only seen him once so far, and I had no idea how long I'd been alone for. There were no windows in the cellar, no way to tell what the time was without a clock or a watch. I hated it. Hated being so fucking dependent on this man who had by all means kidnapped me, and had so far shown zero remorse or desire to release me.

So when I heard the door to the cellar opening again, I got as excited as I did scared. My instinct was to crawl closer to him as soon as he came through, the chain around my ankle preventing me from running or standing up straight. I needed to be comforted, to know he'd take care of me and not just forget he'd locked me in the darkness.

"Come out, come out, wherever you are," he said in a singsong voice, fucking mocking and making me grit my teeth angrily. He chuckled to himself, a low and evil sound coming from deep in his throat.

Our eyes connected, me on the floor, kneeling like a fucking pet for him to play with, and Law standing over me, dominant and demanding, ready to do anything he wanted with me.

"Crawl closer," he told me, setting down a tray of food on the wooden table in the corner. I didn't move, and his expression darkened, like a cloud looming over his handsome features. "I said fucking crawl, babygirl."

"Fuck you." I blurted the two words, glaring at him with all the rage I had left in my body. I hated him for keeping me here, and I hated him more for the reaction my body had to him. I was already wet, feeling my cunt drip between my legs at his mere presence.

"You will," Law said calmly. "Don't worry about that, babygirl. Now crawl fucking closer and be a good little girl before I lose my damn patience."

I stared at him defiantly, my heart beating so loudly I was almost sure he could hear it. I wanted to object and tell him to go to hell, but I couldn't make the words leave my lips. I couldn't move either, even if I'd wanted to, finding myself glued to my spot on the floor. Law's expression darkened even more and I knew that meant trouble.

"Always knew you were a fucking brat," he told me through gritted teeth. "We're gonna have to knock that right out of your system, aren't we?"

I shivered hearing his words, my eyes widening in fear. For some reason I'd been sure Law wouldn't hurt me, but what made me so sure? He'd already proven I couldn't trust him, stealing me from that club. And yet there was a part of me that wanted to trust him so fucking badly I could almost convince myself I'd be safe with him.

He closed in on me, two fucking steps and we were side by side. I whimpered when he grabbed my hair, a strong fist wrapping around its length and yanking me to my feet.

"Stop that," I whined. "That fucking hurts!"

"I know," he replied calmly, his fingers still wrapped around my ratty mane. "I like it when it does, babygirl."

I couldn't help myself and a small moan left my lips, begging him to say more. There was something in the way he talked, like he didn't give a fuck about my status or who I was—something I wasn't familiar with. Money ruled my life, and as soon as anyone found out my name, I could have had anything I wanted.

But Law didn't seem to give a fuck about that. The only thing he cared about was the wetness between my legs, of that, I was sure. I'd seen the way he reacted to my moans, to my legs clamping around his hand.

He fucking wanted me. The question was, how badly and what could I make him do in exchange for my body? The thought turned me on.

I stood up on shaky legs, my eyes turned down and my cheeks blushing deeply. I was only wearing my dress from a few days ago, dirty now. My panties had gotten soaked so many times I felt gross in them.

"I want a shower," I whined. "And I need the bathroom."

"Is that so?" Law asked me. I still wouldn't look at him, but he came closer, grabbing my chin roughly and making me look into his eyes. "Good girls beg pretty, Lily. Show me."

My whole body was shaky as fuck, and maintaining eye contact with him was making me shiver. "Please," I uttered, and a brilliant smile lit up Law's face. "Please let me use the bathroom."

"Not good enough," he growled, and I felt my pressure rising, already feeling pissed off because of the way he was treating me. "Beg nicer, babygirl. I like the word please on your lips."

"Please, just let me," I whispered, my eyes pooling with tears but not because I was scared. They were tears of stubbornness and he was pissing me off. "Please, Law."

He snapped, his hand wrapping around my throat so fast I didn't even have the chance to take my last breath. His eyes zeroed in on mine and I was scared, legitimately scared of the intensity in his gaze.

"Don't use my name," he growled. "I told you as a fucking courtesy. You will always address me as Daddy down here. Is that clear, babygirl?"

I didn't respond, retreating into a small corner of my mind, and it seemed to piss him off. His grip on my throat tightened, making me mewl. "Is that fucking clear?"

"Yes!" I struggled in his firm, unrelenting grasp. He wasn't going to let go, but apparently, my begging had been good enough as he bent down to undo the shackle on my ankle. He set me free.

"And don't even think about running," he said in a voice that was certain I wouldn't. He took my hand and led me to the bathroom that I'd seen the previous day. It wasn't seedy, though it wasn't particularly nice either.

"Toilet's in the corner," he said, his voice hoarse. He turned his back on me as I got up, my shaky legs barely holding me up. He must have taken off my heels, and being barefoot felt disgusting in the grimy old cellar.

I waited for Law to leave, but he wasn't moving. I briefly contemplated attacking him, but I knew I was no match. I was a petite, tiny girl, and he towered over six-and-a-half-feet tall. I wouldn't stand a chance.

I walked over to the horrible toilet in the corner, the one that seemed so disgusting only a couple of hours ago. Now I was looking forward to relieving myself, as horrible as it was compared to my luxurious bathroom at home.

I sat down on the toilet, glancing toward Law. He was half-turned toward me and I felt awkward as hell. I couldn't do this. Not with him staring at me the whole way through.

"Do you mind?" My voice was barely above a hiss, but

instead of turning away, Law looked right at me. I felt vulnerable all of a sudden, sitting on the dingy toilet with all of my parts exposed. Not that he hadn't seen them before, but... There are times when you want privacy, and his mocking look was getting on my nerves.

"Do I mind what?" he asked. I blushed deeply, trying to cover up my modesty, but he still wouldn't look away. However, I could hear his breathing grow heavier, his breaths rapid and urgent now.

"Look away," I said. I'd be lying to myself if I said I wasn't begging at that point.

He defied me, staring at me still. I was furious now. This prick had taken everything away from me, and now he was about to take my dignity, too. But I wasn't fucking having it. I wanted him to be as deeply uncomfortable as I was.

So I looked him right in the eye with a determined expression on my face. He didn't waver. I started to pee, slowly, and cringing the whole way through. But I wouldn't fucking look away. Oh no, I stared right at the prick as I did my business.

I waited for him to break. Waited for him to turn away.

But despite his breathing getting heavier and his cheeks becoming lightly flushed beneath all that stubble, he didn't look away. He kept his eyes on mine while I peed and it made me flush with embarrassment. I still kept my eyes fixed on him, and he did the same.

It was bizarre. Wrong. Fucked up.

It made me feel incredibly dirty.

And I liked it.

Once I was done, Law's cheeks lost their reddish color, his face devoid of emotions once again.

I half-expected him to tie me up again, but he didn't make a move to do so. Instead, he gave me another one of his strange looks.

"I know this place is a dump," he said.

"No shit," I snorted. "I figured it comes with the kidnapping."

Right away, the connection between us was lost and he merely glared at me. "Don't fucking act like you don't belong here," Law growled at me. "This is your fucking home, babygirl."

With that, he tugged on my arm and half-dragged, half-carried me back to the cellar. He didn't stop until we were back; letting go of me so suddenly I just collapsed on the floor. I picked myself up right away, giving him an angry look he didn't acknowledge. He was treating me like a ragdoll, and I wasn't going to let him get away with it.

"I want to go home," I said, aware of the whiny tone of

my voice. "I don't want to be here anymore. Did you send the ransom note? My mom will pay..."

That made him laugh, and my cheeks blushed in response. "You're so fucking naïve, babygirl." He shook his head, a smile playing on his lips. "You think this is about money?"

"Isn't it always?" I asked. It made him shut up and think for a second, but he shook it off pretty fast, leaving me wondering about the sudden change in his attitude.

"You're staying here," he finally said. "You're not going anywhere, baby."

The weight of his words sunk and I felt my bottom lip jut out in protest, hating myself for showing him my weakness, showing him he had an effect on me. I wanted to go home. I wanted to get away. I was sure Law knew but it didn't fucking faze him.

I thought for a second he would leave then; just let me wallow in my self-pity. Maybe that's what he wanted at first, but once he saw the pained expression on my face, he changed his mind.

He came up to me and I backed up in a panic, until he had me pressed right against the wall. He put his palms on the wall on either side of me, caging me in effectively.

"I like you broken."

His voice was low and almost sweet. It made my body respond, my hips pressing up against his and I hated myself for it. It was like I couldn't help myself around this man. My body acted out when he was around.

He grinned at me like a fucking monster, baring his teeth in a smile that was more threatening than it was friendly.

"I want to taste you," Law told me, and I felt my skin prickle at the sound of his words. "I need to put my tongue on your clit, babygirl, have you cum on it."

I felt myself blushing at the crudeness of his words, unable to meet his eyes. He was looking at me with such intensity I had to risk a look into his eyes nonetheless, and the heat in them made me unable to look away.

Before I could respond, he reached for my hips, his fingers digging into my skin there. He hooked his thumbs through my panties and slid them off with a single push, making me gasp out loud.

"Are you dripping yet?" he cooed, his voice sweet and teasing, almost like he was talking to a child. It made me flush deeper, embarrassing me to my core. "Let me see, sweetheart. Let me feel you gush all over my fingers."

I gasped as he slid to his knees in front of me, pushing me against the cool concrete of the wall. I felt grimy and gross, having not had a shower in days now. I'd managed to clean up a little after peeing, but having him this close to me made me terribly self-conscious.

"Your pussy smells fucking divine, babygirl," Law told me in that raspy voice of his. "I bet you taste amazing."

He grabbed my ass with both hands and my hips bucked toward him, my own body betraying me with the need to be closer to his mouth. He buried his face between my legs and I yelped in shock as his beard prickled the sensitive skin there.

Law licked the folds of my cunt and I felt tears burning my eyes, tears of humiliation because I wanted him to do this. I wanted him to bury himself in my cunt and make me cum on his tongue like he'd promised.

A single tear slid down my cheek at the same time a sensual moan escaped my lips. He chuckled at that, and my hands went down instinctively, trying to push him away, my cheeks flushed with embarrassment.

Law grabbed my wrists and held them firmly, making it impossible for me to stop him.

"Are you gonna be a good girl now?" he asked me, and I nodded desperately because I was so fucking vulnerable in that moment I would've done anything he asked of me.

"Let me go." I stuttered over the words, but he didn't even acknowledge them. "Please, let me leave."

"Never," he promised me, and his grip on my wrists

 DADDY'S GIRL | 43

tightened. "I'm gonna let go of you now, babygirl, and you're gonna part your fucking whore legs for me and show me that pretty pussy. Is that fucking clear?"

I whimpered and he squeezed my wrists hard in warning, making me nod deliriously instead. "Yes," I managed to get out.

He did as he promised, letting go of my wrists. He guided my hands gently to my center and they shook as I parted my folds for him, letting him in and showing him a part of me no one had seen yet. He took a sharp breath and sighed.

"So gorgeous," he told me. "And so damn wet for me already. You're a horny little mess as soon as I get my hands on you, aren't you, babygirl?"

I couldn't say a word, too embarrassed and too fucking needy to so much as open my mouth. "Please." It was the only word I could use with him freely, or at least so it seemed.

"You're such a fucking brat," Law growled at me. "Why do you turn so submissive the moment I get my hands on you, hmmm, babygirl?"

I looked away and he slid a finger between my folds, outlining my pussy and making me gasp. Several more tears fell down my cheeks and I bit my lip to stop myself from crying out.

"I think you were made for this," he told me softly. "Made to be a little fucktoy, trained and used however I see fit."

I couldn't help it; his words turned me on. I felt myself getting wetter, so vulnerable under his watchful gaze. "Fuck," Law muttered, his gaze fixed on my dripping cunt. "I'm sorry, baby, I need a taste of you."

He dipped a finger between my pussy lips and I cried, my chest heaving with sobs. Not because I wasn't enjoying it, but because I wanted so much more. For the first time in my life, my pussy burned with the need to be split open, to be owned by an older man like Law. And I couldn't stop myself from saying the word he'd told me to address him with.

"Daddy."

There it was, out in the open, as big and as scary as it had sounded in my mind. Law looked up at me with surprise and I resisted, trying to get away from him, so fucking embarrassed I wished the ground would open up and swallow me whole.

"That's right, sweetheart," he cooed. "Your Daddy's gonna make you cum with his tongue."

He licked my clit then, and I went crazy. My body bucked, desperate to get away from him and closer to his mouth at the same time. He held my hips firmly and I couldn't get away as he started working my pussy with his lips, claiming me one inch of writhing, hot flesh at a time.

"You taste so good," he said into my folds. "So fucking sweet, babygirl."

The change in his demeanor was amazing. He was so strict, almost pissed off with me earlier, but the moment I submitted to him he was so sweet and caring it seemed like he was a different fucking person.

"That hot, tight little pussy needs to cum," he said, and I cried out when his teeth grazed my clit, biting down on the little button and making me curse out loud. "Dirty little mouth. We're gonna take care of that too, don't you worry, sweetheart."

I was still crying, big hot tears of shame falling down my cheeks as Law's tongue brought me closer and closer to an orgasm. I was writhing, shaking, needing him so fucking badly my eyes rolled back in anticipation, my orgasm building deep inside me. I felt it coming down, like a dam breaking open and threatening to flood everything close by.

I was so close. So close I thought I was coming already, and it gave me strength I didn't knew I had in me.

With all my might, I grabbed Law's shoulders and pushed him away. He landed on the floor at the same time I came, my body shaking and moans being ripped from my lips as I held on to the wall and dripped down my own thighs.

Law picked himself up and watched me come before pinning me against the wall. My body went slack, tired and rigid after what he'd put me through.

"You don't get to do that," he told me. "When I want you to cum on my tongue, you fucking obey, sweetheart."

He was a different person now, pissed as fuck that I'd pushed him away. He switched between these two personalities depending on whether I was acting out. One so caring and sweet and the other cruel and relentless.

"You're gonna regret pushing me away," he promised, pushing a sweaty strand of hair off my face. "That was just the fucking warm-up, babygirl. It's your turn to get a taste next time."

I paled, all of the color draining from my face as he grinned at me and backed away. I gripped the wall to hold myself up, vulnerable and exhausted as he gave me one last look before heading for the door.

And then I heard the lock turning, and I was by myself again.

This time, I fucking hated the silence even more.

CHAPTER 5

Law

BEING AWAY FROM HER WAS torture.

For me probably more so than it was for her, but a part of me couldn't help but revel in the knowledge that she had to be hurting too. I had seen it on her face the last time I left her alone. That honest sense of abandonment that wrenched at my heart, making me want to go back and take her in my arms.

But this was for Lily's own good. She had to be strong, and she couldn't be without help. She needed teaching. She needed guiding.

Nothing and no one was allowed to break my Lily but me. And I was going to fucking shatter her, so she could be put together as one again.

"Lawson, dear, must you?" Emily asked as I strode past the kitchen the next day, having barely slept or eaten.

I couldn't concentrate on anything but Lily in the cellar, and I couldn't go to her. My attempts at working and running my company, or distracting myself in general, had been mostly useless. I'd yelled at a lot of people over the last forty-eight hours, and Emily was itching to be the next on the list.

"Must I what?" I asked, forcing the words out of myself as I leaned against the kitchen doorway.

"Must you go down there again?"

"Do you want her to starve? I thought you'd have more heart than that."

I didn't, really, and the look she gave me over her thin-rimmed reading glasses told me the same. I saw the tiny, calculated breath she took, the way her nostrils flared when she got angry, the way she sat up a little straighter. Funny how you get to know a person, regardless of what you think of them as a human being.

"I simply want time with my husband," she said curtly. "Is that too much to ask for?"

By now, her words were draped in sarcasm, and I smirked. She mimicked the smile, but there was no emotion in it, good or foul.

"You and I both know that isn't true," I told her, now moving past her to grab a smoothie and a sandwich from the fridge.

I'd prepared some earlier, during the night. Emily wouldn't touch a slice of bologna if it were the last source of nutrition on the planet.

"I'm telling you to be careful, Lawson," she called after me, her voice and the way she said my name grating on the fiber of my being, like someone was running their carefully manicured nails down a chalkboard.

"I'm telling you that my well-being is none of your fucking business, Emily," I shot back, letting the cellar door fall shut behind me.

I took the stairs quickly and the key to Lily's cell was in my hand far before I reached the door. When I unlocked the door and stepped in, she stirred on the dirty mattress, her hair sticking to her neck and shoulders where the tight party dress didn't hide her from me. Her neck was still tattered with bruises, purple and blue now. They looked like jewels on her.

"I hope I didn't disturb you," I mocked, putting the drink and the sandwich down by the door.

She glanced at them hungrily, but the way she looked at me made ravenous. There was need there, and genuine joy. She bit her lip and averted her gaze, tugging the hem of her dress down a little over her knees.

"You won't hide anything from me," I told her, crossing my arms over my chest. "Come to me."

I stood in the middle of the dark room, legs slightly parted, my hard-on throbbing against my thigh. I loved seeing her on her knees, on the floor, dirty and filthy and so ready for me. She moved to stand up tentatively and I raised my hand, stopping her.

"No. Just like you are right now."

Lily frowned, but realized what I meant. I could see the way she was swallowing hard, the way the tears were brimming in her eyes. And I caught the exact moment she decided to behave.

Good girl.

Touching her palms down on the ground, she crawled across the short expanse to me, her eyes down. Her blonde hair, tattered now, hung about her like a drape of shame. She crawled right up to me and then stopped, falling back on her ankles and heels. She was sobbing soundlessly, but she'd come to me, the ankle chain clattering the whole time like a soundtrack to her shame.

I put a finger under her chin and lifted it gently,

making her look up at me. She stole a glance at the throbbing thickness in my pants, and I had to force down the grin, all of Emily's bullshit promptly forgotten.

"Did you miss me, babygirl?"

She nodded.

"Say it."

"Yes, Daddy."

Fuck, hearing her say those words sent my heart soaring. The memory that came right along with it was bittersweet, but faded quickly next to the blue eyes staring up at me.

"Good girl," I said, reveling in the words.

The nervous smile that lit her face seemed to make the whole room brighter. She glanced at my cock again and her fingers played with the hem of her dress. She was nervous. Needy. Scared. It all looked gorgeous on her.

Absently, I let my free hand run over my cock, grabbing it through the fabric of my pants. She gasped, recoiling slightly. My eyes narrowed and she knew she'd fucked up, righting herself quickly in that way she had, her spine perfectly rigid. Like someone had spent a lifetime smacking her between the shoulder blades, telling her to sit proper.

"Good girls get rewarded," I told her, rubbing my thumb over the head of my cock, barely restraining a groan.

I hadn't touched myself since I saw her stepping off that train. I wanted her to get all of my cum, all of my fucking seed. It was hers now and she hadn't even realized it yet. It felt like I would explode if I couldn't claim her sweet little mouth right then and there, the quiver of her lower lip driving me out of my mind.

She watched, mesmerized, as I undid the buckle of my belt, followed by the button and the zipper on the pants. I took my time, stroking my rigid cock through my black boxers, before pulling it out for her. It sprang out right next to her pretty face, the veins thick and hard and the cut head aching to be thrust between her lips.

Slowly, I ran my hand over it again, and she watched it, her mouth falling open a little like in a trance. I'd dreamed of this moment, her shy face marred with warring emotions, knowing she shouldn't want this as bad as she did, the way her breath hitched telling me more than she probably wanted me to know.

So ripe, so fucking ready.

I slapped the head against her cheek and she yelped, twitching away again. She could barely move an inch before I had my hand fisted in her hair yanking her back and rubbing my cock against her face with the other hand.

"Lawson!" she shrieked, panicking.

"I told you not to call me that," I growled, but her hysteria only made me harder.

Precum beaded on the tip of my cock and I spread it around her mouth, even though she was trying to close her lips. It left a pearly sheen on her lips, like she'd just put on lip gloss, the filthy fucking whore.

"Open your mouth," I told her, grinding out the words.

Her eyes were shining with tears as she looked up at me, desperate and confused. I knew she wanted this as much as I did, but the fucking brat had to have her own way. It made it better, though. Easy victories were never as fun as the hard-fought ones.

With my hand in her hair, holding her tight enough to hurt even if she stood perfectly still, I waited. She stared at me with what I imagined had to be defiance, but a little girl on her knees in a grimy cellar was hardly inspiring respect. My cock twitched in my hand and against her cheek and I couldn't help myself from smacking her hand again with it. She shuddered so beautifully when I did that.

I didn't say a word, until she closed her eyes and opened her mouth. I bit my tongue, reveling in the sweet sight of her virgin mouth. Slowly, I guided the head of my cock to her lips.

"Lick it, babygirl," I said, my tone softer now.

I loved it when she behaved.

Cautiously, she peeked out her tongue and when it touched the head of my cock, I groaned, loosening my hold on her hair a little. Bolstered by it, she licked across the head and got her first taste of precum. I caught the exact moment when her eyes lit up, the salty taste hitting her taste buds. I knew right then and there that she would be a good cumslut. She just needed time... and discipline.

"Good girl," I whispered, and she licked me again, this time lapping more hungrily.

Her eyes lidded slightly and she lost herself in the moment, pleasuring her Daddy's cock. Shy, careful, unsure of herself, but she was doing it. She was doing exactly what she was told and I felt like I could rule the fucking world right then and there.

"Take it in your mouth," I instructed her.

She hesitated again, stopping mid-motion, her tongue flat against the crown of the head. A shadow of a frown crossed over her features and my fingers twisted in her hair, irritation brimming in me.

"Are you being a bad girl again?" I asked tersely.

And there was my fucking brat again. She opened her mouth wide and took the huge head in. I caught her just as she was starting to bite down, her pearly white teeth wanting to rip at the flesh of my cock. I yanked her back and away from myself, cringing as her teeth grazed my flesh, leaving red marks and almost drawing blood.

"You fucking bitch," I hissed, throwing her away from me.

She fell back with a clatter of the chain around her ankle following her, gasping as her body hit the cold concrete.

"You don't get to tell me what the fuck I have to do," she growled, the little hellcat.

I saw red. Seething, but harder than fucking ever, I tucked my cock back in the boxers and zipped up my pants. With one smooth motion, I pulled the belt off my hips and wrapped it around my hand once, watching her the entire time.

Lily was crawling back against the wall, her back to it, her knees pulled to her chest. She was staring at me with confusion and anger, but I knew a part of her was hating herself. Hating the fact that she hadn't been a good girl for me. Hating that she hadn't done what I knew she *needed* to do. She needed my cock. Just as fucking much as I needed her lips wrapped around it.

"Are you going to punish me now?" she mocked, but her voice shook.

My lips hardened to a thin line. I crossed the room to

her and grabbed her by the arm, painfully pulling her to her feet. She screamed, terror and anger in her voice, as I dragged her to the chair in the middle of the room. I sat down, letting go of her hand.

"Get down. Over my knees," I told her, my voice allowing for no disobedience.

She stared at me, shivering all over, as if shocked that I was actually going to go through with it.

"Now," I added, feeling the muscles in my arms clench. "Do as you're told."

I gave her that moment again. That second to make up her mind whether she was going to be bad or good for me, whether she was going to make it hard for herself or not. Finally, she relented, tears freely falling down her cheeks now as she gingerly got down on her stomach on my legs.

The weight of her petite body felt like nothing, but my insides burned as she draped herself over me, shaking like a leaf. I smoothed my hand over the back of her bare thighs and she moaned audibly, fear and lust all in one. Moving up, I pulled the dress over her bare ass and ran two fingers along her wet slit. She was so fucking turned on, my filthy girl.

Memories of doing this again and again wanted to come to me, and I had to steel myself against them. She looked so much like...

No.

Not now.

Wetting my lips, I wrapped the belt around my right hand now, and then let the buckle slide up and down the back of her thighs a few times. Lily went completely rigid, suspended in time.

"Please," she begged, and I knew she was asking me to not do it.

I bet no one had disciplined her spoiled ass in all her life. She would have to learn to cope with my fucking belt.

"Please what?" I asked, smacking her on the ass lightly with the flat of my hand, the leather of the belt only lightly licking the cheeks of her pale, perfect ass.

"Please don't hurt me... Daddy," she whispered, looking over her shoulder at me.

I suppressed a grin.

"You hurt Daddy, babygirl," I said sternly. "You're going to have to pay the price for your stupid fucking mouth."

That's when I raised my hand again and this time, I let the leather and the buckle of the belt hit her right on her ass. She tensed, the air getting stuck in her lungs, and she didn't scream before I did it another time. I flattened my free palm on her lower back, holding her still over my knees as I hit her again, careful not to let the belt hit her exposed cunt.

"Daddy!" she squealed through blubbery tears, pain breaking her voice.

My cock throbbed painfully against her belly as she called for me, shivering, but I wouldn't stop. I hit her again.

And again.

And again, the belt leaving red welts and the buckle scratching her ass. My hand moved lower, slashing one across her thighs, and she screamed like the world was going to end.

"Daddy, please!" she wailed, thrashing in my lap. "No, please! I'll be good!"

I ignored her. In my head, I counted to ten. When I hit her for the eleventh time, she stilled slightly. Her screams were just as loud, but her body learned to expect them. The endorphins had to be kicking in, flooding her body. The fifteenth hit, across her thighs again, was the last one.

I let the belt drop from my hand and placed my palm on her ass, warm and pink and definitely sore. She whimpered, the coolness of my palm having to feel good. I ran my hand lower, across her thighs, and then up to her pussy again.

"Shit, babygirl," I whispered, spreading her lips with two fingers and running my middle finger up and down her slit. "You're wet for Daddy, aren't you?"

She didn't answer me, only biting her lip, her face red and blotchy with tears and her breathing still heavy. I bundled her up in my arms, twisting her around and cradling her against my chest for a moment. I wanted nothing more than to fill that bratty cunt of hers with my cock right then and there.

I held her only long enough for her heart to stop pounding in her chest like it was about to pop out. Then, I pushed her off without warning, picked up my belt and made for the door. The keys jangled in my hands as I pulled them out of my pants pocket.

"You have to be better next time, babygirl," I told her as I unlocked the door.

She didn't answer.

She'd learn her manners soon enough.

CHAPTER 6

Lily

HE WAS INTENT ON BREAKING me.

The way he'd punished my ass, the red welts still reminding me of what he called disobedience, was cruel and evil. And I hated that I got wetter with every hit of the leather across my backside.

I don't know what had gotten into me when I bit down on his cock. I knew I couldn't overpower him anyway, but I needed to fight back. It wasn't because I hated what he was doing. It was because I needed to know I still had some control.

Time passed excruciatingly slowly when he left me

to rot in the cellar. I had no idea of what time of the day it was. The only hint of the hours passing were the trays with food that appeared when I slept.

I knew Law had to be coming down when I was sleeping, but I never once caught him doing so. The meals were far and few between, so I figured he was only bringing them once per day. Another part of my punishment.

My body started burning up as time passed. I wasn't sure whether it was a fever or the anger simmering right under my skin. I resented Law for leaving me down there, but I was getting more and more desperate for him to come back.

I would've done anything to bring him back.

To feel his lips against mine again.

To call him Daddy and blush at the forbidden word, pretending it didn't make me drip down my legs.

I retreated into my head. Ignored my surroundings, ate the sandwiches he brought me like I was on autopilot, and drank the water obediently. I didn't scream– I knew I'd deserved my punishment. But I cried a lot, hot tears burning lines down my cheeks and stinging my skin.

I didn't know what day it was when I started hearing my mother's voice through the walls, but when I did, I knew I was going fucking crazy.

It wasn't clear, and afterward I could only remember snippets of what I'd imagined her saying. But it was definitely her, and I realized I would lose my mind if Lawson didn't come back soon.

My dreams were plagued by my mother's voice, my thoughts peppered with images of Law's dick pushing into my mouth. I needed him back. Almost more so than I needed to get the fuck out of the cellar.

When I heard the locks in the door turning, my heart surged. It was Law—my punishment was finally over.

He didn't need to tell me to crawl to him this time around. The moment the door flew open, I was on my knees, making my way to his feet. I was too shaken up to look into his eyes, so I focused my gaze on the leather of his boots instead.

"I see you've learned some manners," Law said softly, his voice dark and promising a world of trouble if I misbehaved again. "Good fucking girl."

I whimpered, wanting to address him the way he told me to, but I couldn't bring myself to do it. Instead, I braced my palms on the floor and leaned down against his feet. Something came over me, and my lips brushed the dark leather of his shoes in a silent kiss.

"What a little overachiever," Law grunted, and I

found myself blushing. Finally, I risked taking a look into his eyes. They were troubled, hiding secrets from me, but at the same time, I could tell he was holding himself back.

I'd stripped off my dress that morning. The cellar wasn't hot, but the fever was burning me up.

Law's hand brushed my cheek and I leaned into it, hating myself for breaking so easily. I told myself I was only doing it to get in his good graces, but I think we both knew the truth. I needed Lawson.

"Get on my boot, babygirl," he told me gently, the edge in his voice slowly dissipating and being replaced by genuine affection. "Ride it."

I blushed and hesitated for a second, long enough to make his eyes cloud over. He grabbed my chin, making me look at him.

"I said fucking now," he growled at me, and I felt the familiar hint of tears prickling in my eyes. "You don't want to be punished again, do you, baby?"

I shook my head no and pulled my body over his boot, settling my naked pussy over the shoe. He groaned as I looked up at him, my eyes wide with expectation. We both knew what was coming next.

He tangled one hand in my hair, his fingers twisting into knots in my blonde mane. I took a deep breath when he reached for his zipper, undoing it in a single motion. Law pulled out his cock.

It was even fucking bigger than I remembered; so huge I couldn't even imagine fitting it in my mouth. I doubted I could even wrap my lips around the thick bulging head again, but I knew I would have to.

"Come on, babygirl." Law's voice had lost its edge again, and I noticed the same note of affection he'd used with me before when I was being good. "Open that pretty little mouth of yours and stick out your tongue for Daddy."

I didn't want to obey at first, but his words had a strange effect on me and my lips parted as if of their own accord. I stuck out my tongue, feeling my mouth water involuntarily at the sight of him.

The tip of Law's cock was glistening with what I now knew was precum, decorating his rock hard cock like a single pearl on the tip of it.

A sinister smile took over his face as he stroked my cheek, ready to deal another blow.

"Beg," he told me simply.

My eyes fluttered open and closed and I swallowed thickly, but the lump in my throat wouldn't go away. I knew this was coming, knew he would take it a step further just to punish me some more for biting him the last time he was down here.

"Please," I choked out, the word barely above a whisper.

He raised his eyebrows at me and I sobbed, my chest heaving with the silent plea to make him stop. The worst part of Law's torture was knowing I liked it, loved the way he made me blush and loved the things he made me do. It made me feel so dirty, so fucking good.

He didn't need to say another word to let me know I'd need to do more than the single please I'd uttered so far. And we both knew I'd be forced to do it eventually, if I didn't want to be left to rot in the cellar by myself again.

My hips started moving then, rolling over his boots and making me gasp softly as I felt the buttery leather rubbing against my clit. Law's grip on my hair tightened, and a look in his eyes told me he was surprised, but pleased with what I was doing. It felt too good to stop, what was supposed to distract him lighting a fire inside me.

"Please, Daddy." The word fell off my lips with more ease now, and I blushed deeply as my eyes connected with his. "Please, let me suck your cock clean."

"Good girl," Law cooed, smoothing down my hair though his grip was still tight and unrelenting. I couldn't get away from him, and I didn't want to anymore, either. "See what a few days of solitude can teach you? I don't like brats, baby. We're gonna have to turn you into a good little girl for Daddy."

I moaned, my hips sliding across his boot and covering it in my juices. I was wetter than I'd ever been and so fucking desperate. Law stroked himself and I licked my lips, needing it inside my mouth. I felt empty, the absence of his bulging cock between my lips almost painful.

He didn't push his cock into my mouth this time. He waited for me to look up at him desperately instead, my tongue out and my chin shaking as I begged silently to be fed.

I finally couldn't take any more. I leaned closer and sucked the tip of him between my lips, filling my mouth with his warmth. The salty taste made me shiver and I mewled against his dick as I sucked clumsily.

"Just like that, babygirl," Law told me with a groan. He yanked on my hair and I yelped when he pushed my head back, making his cock go that much deeper inside my mouth. He filled me completely, going so deep I almost choked, filling my whole throat with his hardness.

"Good fucking girl," Law said. "Open wider."

I obeyed, my eyes going to his and begging. Not for him to stop, but for more.

I started sucking at the same time as my tongue slid across his length, licking every inch of Law's cock and tasting his musk on my lips. My hips started grinding against his boot again, picking up speed as I sucked, getting more and more desperate to get myself off. My hands shook and I fought the instinct to reach between my legs, push down on my clit and make myself cum.

Law noticed, and his grin made me flush.

"Does my baby want to get off?" he asked me sweetly. There was an edge to his voice and I knew he was getting close to blowing his hot load inside my mouth. "Go on then, princess. Reach between those whore legs and strum your clit for me. Show me how you play for Daddy."

I obeyed because I needed to. The desire to cum along with him was making me tense, and as soon as my fingers touched my clit, I moaned, a long and sensual sound that made his cock slide deeper between my lips.

Law groaned and I started touching myself. I wasn't used to touching myself like that, having always been too shy to get myself off. But with him watching me, it was easier, and my fingers fell into rhythm along with the thrusts of Law's hips guiding his cock deeper inside me.

"Jesus fuck, babygirl," he grunted. "Cum with me. You need to cum for Daddy."

I moaned, slow and deep and needy as he started fucking my mouth. I had stopped sucking, too needy to get myself off to pay any attention to the cock between my lips.

"Don't you fucking dare stop sucking," Law snapped.

"Keep licking, baby. Keep getting yourself off until Daddy blows his hot load inside your mouth."

I could barely obey, so far gone, so needy for the release I'd been working toward I almost forgot to flick my tongue against the silky skin of Law's cock. I felt him tighten, felt him throb on my tongue right before he came, cursing out loud and spilling every drop of his hot seed down my throat.

His dick was lodged so deep inside my throat I didn't even need to swallow. His cum slid down my throat and I lapped at his cock desperately for another taste just as the orgasm took over, making me shake and leak all over Law's boot.

He was pulling on my hair hard as his dick slowly softened in my mouth. I felt hot shameful tears sliding down my cheeks as I came down from my high, crawling off of his boot, Law's dick slipping from my mouth with a loud slurp.

Lawson gave me a moment, never letting go of my hair as he took a deep breath and watched the sobs shake my body. For a second I thought I'd heard my mom's voice again, the phantom sound of it echoing in my head.

"What a good fucktoy," Lawson told me, stroking my hair off my face. "Now be an even better little slut and lick yourself off Daddy's boot."

I gave him an incredulous look, ready to bite back a reply, but his eyes told me everything I needed to know. This was another test, and I needed to pass it if I wanted this to go back to the way they were—the new normal.

Slowly, I got on my hands and knees and my tongue slipped out between my lips. I licked at the leather tentatively, one slow flick of my tongue after the other. Law's hand remained tangled in my hair as he crouched down and he petted me like a kitten as I cleaned my own juices off.

I forgot to feel embarrassed.

I forgot to complain, or bitch, or be a little brat.

I licked the last trace of my orgasm off his boots, and he grinned at me, looking prouder than ever.

"Good girl," he said, kissing my shaking lips and groaning when he tasted the mix of our juices on my mouth. "Such a good little girl for Daddy."

CHAPTER 7

Law

I WETTED MY LIPS, LEANING BACK in the wide, high-backed leather chair in my office. Kicking my feet up on the desk, I frowned, deep in thought.

Somewhere deeper in the house, I could hear Emily walking around, the clatter of her high heels making my lips turn in a slight sneer. With every day that Lily spent under this roof, I found myself despising Emily more. It was a skill I had long imagined myself a master of.

Reaching for the tumbler of whiskey on the table, I sloshed the golden liquid tentatively around in the glass a few times before taking a sip. It went down smooth and fast, burning just right in my throat. I hadn't drank since... well, since. It was one of many rediscovered firsts that I found myself enjoying, even while my irritation with Emily rose almost as if to counteract it.

My fingers thrummed on the armrest in a steady rhythm, a physical representation of the stirred, nervous energy within me. Every second I wasn't down in the basement with Lily was one that felt wasted. Every moment that I couldn't lavish her with attention seeming to be spent frivolously.

Patience, I reminded myself tiredly, setting the glass down.

The days when I'd had to stay away from her had gone past torturously slowly, hours dragging like years. Yet I felt more alive when I had to wait for her to learn than I had in the last years.

My eyes tracked the outlines of her smile on the pictures plastered on the wall, some put up there repeatedly, taken from her Instagram feed, or Facebook, or other means of careless social media. The image that she painted of herself to the world was one of a spoiled brat, a young woman who thought her worth was defined by the purses she owned and the clothes she wore. I doubted she'd ever really considered that there could be anything else about her worth showing or thinking about.

The question of how she had gotten that way had never crossed my mind. Was it even important?

Probably not, I thought, practically scoffing as I found myself reaching for the whiskey again.

This time, I downed the remainder of it, letting it scorch down my throat and take my troubled thoughts with me.

Besides, it was evident enough to me what had made her like this. Not just too much money and a lack of any discernible structure in her life, but eager confirmation from the world around her that she was the best version of herself that she could be. She'd never had a man in her life who told her how to be better, how to be a good little girl.

She'd never had a Daddy.

I had been looking for someone like her for so long. It still sent a tingle down my spine, thinking of the lengths I had to go to in order to have her.

Checking the time on my phone, I stood up, tucking the smartphone away in my back pocket, next to the keys to the cellar. It was a set of three, one for the bathroom, one for the cell, and then the last one for the cellar itself, which was left unlocked.

I stood up, the telltale sounds of Emily's high heels making a beeline for the office smoothing away whatever positive thoughts that had been brewing within me. She had a way of doing that, ruining even the anticipation of seeing my little pet. We met at the doorway to my office, catching her when she was just raising her hand to knock, opening the door before she could.

Emily's cold, regal face twisted in an awkward smile. She had her hair down this time, platinum blonde, and she wore a Hermes scarf that probably cost more than the monthly salary of most people.

"Greeting me at the door, how nice of you," she cooed, batting her lashes in a manner that had become all too familiar to me now.

I said nothing in response, pushing past her and pulling the door shut behind me. Walking toward the kitchen, I didn't bother acknowledging her with more than a grunt, prompting her to get on with whatever it was that she'd come to me for.

She had a tendency of seeking me out at the worst times. Like she could somehow sense when I wanted to see her the least, which truthfully was just about always.

"You could at least listen when I have something to tell you," she said with an annoyed sigh as I stocked up the tray I used to take food down to Lily on.

"We discussed this. After she arrives, I need a few weeks with her before anything else can happen."

"It's been a week," Emily said, a certain note of annoyance tinting her words now.

A trait she was not alone in possessing.

"I am not done," I retorted.

Truthfully, I wasn't sure if I'd ever be *done* with Lily, but I was more than certain that there wasn't a thing in the world that Emily could spring upon me now that she was here that would distract me from my babygirl. Though the woman had made it more than evident that she was determined to use whatever power she had over me now that the object of my affections had finally been made mine.

"I understand that," Emily said, her tone almost placating now. "Is it going well? Is she being a *good girl?*" Emily asked, no mockery in her words, but my grip on the plate I was grabbing from the freezer still tightened.

I didn't want anyone talking about her, least of all Emily. Taking a breath that came out more like a growl than anything else, I pulled the food out, set it on the tray and closed the fridge. She leaned against the counter expectantly, a simper on her face. I still couldn't believe she was enjoying this as much as she was.

I'd thought it insane when I approached her the first time about Lily, figuring she would call me a pervert and a monster and a fucking beast. Instead, she'd welcomed me with open arms.

Sometimes I had to wonder who the real monster in this sham of a marriage really was.

"It is none of your business, Emily," I said calmly, flicking her a look that should have shut her up once and for all.

The brazen bitch cocked a fucking brow at me.

"I think you should know that it is," she said, jutting her chin out and crossing her arms over her chest. "She is always going to be my business."

I could feel myself snapping before my brain caught up with it. The next thing I knew, my hand was curled around her long neck, pushing her back so her back arched over the countertop. Her eyes, blue, went wide in her head, reminding me of a more callous version of my babygirl. It was almost enough to make me stop.

"She will never again be your business, Emily," I seethed, squeezing.

Her hands, with her tastefully manicured French-tipped fingers, clutched at my outstretched arm, but she didn't claw at me. If anything, she was way too fucking calm about this whole thing. Her breaths came in ragged heaves as I waited, her lips parting.

She couldn't say anything, but I wanted to see the realization in her eyes, the knowing that she'd fucked up and that she wasn't allowed to do so again. It never came.

When her lips started turning blue from the lack of oxygen, I let go, feeling like I'd just dropped a dead fish. She breathed in a few times, shallow and wheezing, and hunched over slightly, trying to gather herself. Other than her body being ravaged, it looked like she had barely noticed what I did to her.

The woman must have had ice in her veins.

I grabbed the tray and turned to leave, blood boiling in my veins. I knew I couldn't go to Lily like this. She didn't deserve to be punished for my foul mood.

"Careful, Lawson. Or she'll end up just like the last one," Emily hissed from behind me.

Looking over my shoulder, I saw the glare she gave me, vicious and decisive. Any sane man would have counted his blessings to be putting distance between himself and a woman with so much obvious wrath within her.

I considered whether I should go back and finish the job. I'd done worse things to better people.

"We had an agreement, Emily. I expect you to stick to your part, and I will stick to mine," I told her coldly, a sneer plastered on my lips.

She simply straightened up, her neck blotched where I held her. For once, she had the decency not to say a fucking thing about it.

CHAPTER 8

Lily

THE CELLAR WAS MAKING ME feel more and more claustrophobic as the days passed. It felt like the walls were starting to close in on me, holding me captive and suffocating me as if someone had wrapped their fingers around my throat and choked me.

Law had been downstairs every day, sometimes even more than once. He'd brought me some clothes as well, a simple dress that was too short to be modest. He hadn't brought me any underwear to go with it, and I knew better than to argue with him about it.

I was getting antsy, not only because I wanted to leave

the cellar, but because Law hadn't made a move to fuck me yet. After realizing he wasn't going to ask for ransom for me, I figured that was the main reason he'd taken me, and I struggled to understand why the hell he didn't just get on with it.

Especially for the last few times he'd come downstairs, I'd been needy and snippy with him, which resulted in several welts decorating my ass. Law had barely touched me other than that, aside from stroking my hair or cupping my cheek, and it was driving me up the wall.

So I came up with a plan.

The next time he would come down, I'd be ready for him. I'd play him the way he played me, push him so much he would do anything to get off. And then I'd ask for him to let me go.

I ignored the nagging thought in the back of my mind telling me I wasn't even sure whether I really wanted to leave anymore.

The moment I heard the key turning in the lock, I was on my knees. My gaze was trained on the floor like I'd been taught, and when I heard the sounds of his approaching footsteps, I crawled closer to his feet. My ass was up in the air, swaying from left to right as I glided across the floor toward Law.

I settled next to his feet, leaning down coyly and

leaving a fleeting kiss against the leather of his boots.

"What's gotten into you today, babygirl?" he muttered to himself, his hand going to the top of my head and caressing me softly. "You're never usually this good."

I looked up at him, my eyes big and bright and so very fake it almost hurt to giggle playfully. But I still did it, ignoring the pang in my chest telling me there was something there, as much and as hard as I tried to deny it.

There was an attraction between us, something wild and unpredictable and sweet at the same time, that I was still trying to deny existed.

"I have a special treat for you today," he told me wickedly, and I glanced to his feet to find a bucket with steaming, soapy water beside him. My eyes lit up with excitement and Lawson guided me to my feet, leading me to the chair in the room and sitting me down.

"I know I've been mean to you, babygirl," he said with some regret. "It's just the way things have to be right now, sweetheart. But I'm not a complete jackass, you know."

As he was talking, he gently pulled the dress he'd brought me a few days prior over my head and I gasped when I was left naked, covering up my tits and pussy.

Law smiled at me fondly and slapped my hand away. The motion was gentle but firm, and he made me reveal myself to him even though I hadn't been planning on it.

He took the bucket and soaked a sponge inside it, the soft surface of it dripping with the soapy water and making me crave the washing he'd so carefully prepared. He inched closer to me and I sighed when the sponge hit my skin.

Law lathered my skin with the soap, washing away the grimy traces of the cellar. It felt good, really damn good, to be taken care of that way. He'd mostly been rough with me, but I found myself liking this new version, gentler and sweeter.

He washed me carefully, washing away every trace of dirt and grime from my body. I moaned when he was working my tits, making my nipples tighten into pretty, pink buds. When he got his hands between my legs, I was thankful he was washing me, or he would've noticed how wet I was getting from his circular motions.

But Law gave me a knowing smile, and I had a feeling he knew. It made me blush.

"See, sweetheart?" he asked me gently. "Daddy can be good to you as well."

I giggled and pressed my cunt against his hand when he was washing me. I tried to convince myself I was only doing this to get out of here, not wanting to admit the sordid truth to myself.

I wanted him.

Wanted this.

Wanted him to take care of me like no one else had.

Wanted him to fuck me, even if it meant I'd never get the hell out of this damn cellar.

He gave me a quick look and then pushed a finger against my folds, only a little, but enough to make me groan out loud. I wriggled against his hand, trying desperately to get off from the pathetic amount of friction he was giving me.

"Slow down," he muttered against my hair. "Everything in due time, baby."

I let him finish washing me without complaint. When he was done with my body, he washed my hair too, rinsing it out with the now lukewarm water from the bucket. He'd even brought a brush with him, and I stared at him as he combed through my hair, sitting on his knee now.

"Why are you doing this?" I asked, because I couldn't hold back any longer.

He gave me an indulgent look, but it only made me blush in anger.

"Why are you being nice to me?" I demanded. "You don't have to wash me, or take care of me. Just take what you want."

Law laughed out loud, saying: "When I fuck you,

sweetheart, you're going to be begging for it, not telling me to take what I want."

I pursed my lips, sincerely doubting his words. I could never want a man like him, someone so intent on breaking me. I was going to tell him as much... but I knew better than that, so I just shut my mouth instead.

Law didn't stop until I was squeaky clean, and when he took away the bucket and sponge, I felt strangely empty and alone. He was back a moment later with a big, fresh blanket. He wrapped me up in it and guided me to the mattress in the corner.

"I've been thinking," he said. "I want to make this place a little nicer for you. What do you think, babygirl? I could bring you a mirror, maybe. Some pillows. Maybe a book?"

I didn't know whether to laugh or cry, and he seemed to notice right away.

"What's wrong?"

I sniffled. He didn't sound cross, more curious about my inner turmoil. For once, I decided to let him in and explain why I felt this way.

"It sounds like you're planning on keeping me here longer," I said in a small voice. "Like I'm going to spend a very, very long time in this cellar. Like I'm going to be here forever."

I'd be lying if a tiny, sordid part of me didn't like that idea, though.

He brushed a strand of hair off my face and gave me a thoughtful look.

"You wouldn't like that?" he inquired, and I gave him a lost look.

I wasn't even sure what I wanted at that point. I just needed to get some focus, stop being so damn confused.

I felt a tear slide down my cheek and I bit my bottom lip to stop myself from crying out.

Law's finger slid over my lips and I opened my mouth. He slipped his thumb between my lips and I sucked on it gently, needing him to make this better.

"Fuck," he muttered. "I love it when you cry, babygirl."

His words should've made me angry, but instead, they made my pussy throb with some kind of need I barely recognized. This... thing between us, it was primal, like my body responded to Law's demands without me wanting it to happen.

His fingers left my lips and ventured down my chest, under the blanket he'd wrapped around me. He groaned.

"Let me see your body, baby," he muttered.

I hesitated, but only for a second. I needed to remember my goal.

I let the blanket, now a little wet from the contact

with my skin, fall to the floor. I was standing in front of Law completely naked, short and heaving breasts making my chest rise and fall. My hands went to my pussy on instinct, but Law pried them away gently.

"You will not hide what's mine, sweetheart," he told me. "Part your pussy for me, I want to see how wet you are."

I thought I didn't want to do it, but my body did. My fingers trembled as I parted my legs, gently opening my pussy up to his gaze. He groaned, and I could see how swollen his cock had gotten in his jeans when he stretched his hands.

In that moment, with his shirt riding up like that, I saw a set of keys on his belt, and my eyes lit up. I looked away as fast as I could, and I didn't think he'd noticed a thing as I mewled and dropped to my knees in front of him.

"What's this?" he asked bemusedly, and I tried to hide my blushing cheeks by rubbing against his jeans. "What a little slut you are, Lily. You want to please your daddy?"

All I could think about was the set of keys at his belt. How badly I wanted it. How very close to my reach it was now.

I nodded, giving him a smile as I reached for his belt buckle, desperate to undo it.

He grabbed my throat faster than I could yell for help. He lifted me off the floor until my feet dangled, and small, pathetic sounds escaped my throat.

"You think you can get my keys, sweetheart?" Law asked me, his voice pleasant and a sharp contrast to what he was doing with me. "Think again. Now you're getting punished."

He threw me down on the mattress and I started shaking all over as I backed up into the corner. Tears of humiliation fell from my eyes but I was wet. Dripping. I wanted him to punish me in whatever way he chose.

I sobbed out loud as he advanced on me, like a predator hunting down his prey. I felt vulnerable with nothing on, and he was still fully clothed. He caught me in his arms fast, and laid me down surprisingly gently.

"Why are you crying, babygirl?" he asked me roughly, his hand going to the bulge in his jeans.

"I..." I hiccupped when another sob took over my body. "I..."

He merely grinned at me.

"It's ok," he cooed. "I like you so much better in tears, sweetheart."

His words made me let out a soft little sound, something between a gasp and a very, very needy moan. It made

Law's eyes widen, and he guided my hand over the bulge in his jeans.

"Feel that, babygirl?" he asked me. "That's all for you. But I'm not going to fuck you just yet."

"Please," I said, the word barely above a whisper.

"Please?" He was mocking me, laughing out loud at how fucking pathetic I sounded. "Please and what else?"

I didn't understand it, the sudden need to have him inside me. All I knew was, I had to see his cock, feel it on my fingertips. I wanted this to be my fucking choice, not something he'd rip away from me like everything else he'd stolen.

I wanted him.

And god, how I hated him for it.

"Please take your cock out, Daddy," I said in a shaky voice.

It was still weird calling him Daddy, but at the same time, it felt so good.

I remembered my own father, how I lost him when I was so young, but I managed to push the memory away every time. Something about this place though, this damn cellar, made the memory resurface too often for my liking.

Law was serious now, grunting as he undid the zipper on his jeans and slid them down along with his boxers.

His huge cock sprang free, so hard and so bulging it looked red and purple in the dim light of the cellar.

"And your shirt, Daddy, please."

My voice was getting huskier. I ate him up with my eyes, worshipping every inch of his muscled body and that thick cock, hard for me and only me.

He obliged and got on the bed with me, only inches away. I followed his hand to where it was on his cock, and watched him spread the pearl of precum on his tip all over his cock. Lust like I'd never known it took over my body.

"Daddy," I murmured. "Are you going to fuck my little virgin hole now?"

He groaned and ran a hand through his hair. For a second, he looked vulnerable. Really fucking vulnerable, with his face conflicted and his hands shaking like he wasn't sure about this, like he wished he could go back and change things. But it was a fleeting moment.

"Beg," he ordered in a low voice.

I lay back on the mattress, my eyes following his as I spread my legs as wide as I could, baring my pussy to him and moaning softly as I slipped a finger between the lips of my cunt.

"Daddy, please," I said softly. "I want you to fuck me now, right here..."

I circled my clit and cried out. It made him throb so hard his hand shook on his cock.

"I want you to make me a big girl," I went on, blushing deep at the naughty words leaving my lips. "I want to be a good girl and make Daddy cum inside me."

"Jesus, Lily." He just stared at me, his eyes worried, and it riddled me with self-doubt.

"I'm... I'm sorry," I said softly. "I thought... you'd like it."

Feeling self-conscious as hell, I closed my legs and tried to move away, but he grabbed me and pulled me back in front of him.

"I'm not some kind of monster," he told me.

I wasn't sure whether he was trying to convince me or himself. I merely nodded, feeling another tear slip down my cheek.

"I'll only do this if you want me to," he promised me. "Tell me now, sweetheart. Do you want Daddy to fuck you? Do you want Daddy to be your first?"

I was buzzing with need, and my eyes were almost glazed over as I nodded. Once, twice, I couldn't stop. I just nodded.

He put a hand around my waist and laid me down, and it was as if his sweet persona evaporated into thin air the second he did that. I looked between my legs, my soaked little cunt being prodded open by the meaty head of his cock. I almost changed my mind, almost told him no, but in the next second, he was splitting me open.

He forced himself inside me with no grace whatsoever, ramming his cock so deep I cried out in pain.

"Good little girl," he muttered against my ear. "Such a good girl for Daddy."

He moved with purpose and my eyes rolled back as pain ripped through me.

"Oh, babygirl," he cooed. "Look at that, not a virgin anymore."

I gasped as he fucked me deeper, opening my pussy in ways I couldn't even have imagined.

"Your little pussy feels so good on Daddy's cock," Law groaned in my ear. "Fuck, sweetheart, you have the sweetest, tightest little snatch."

He wouldn't stop and I almost passed out from the intensity, not the pain. It only took a couple of thrusts to make me moan, and he laughed at me like a fucking animal as I wriggled on his cock.

"This is the last fucking time I fuck you on a bed," he groaned in my ear. "Makes the thrusts too soft."

His words made me moan and I suddenly couldn't

hold back, the orgasm I'd been clinging to desperately being ripped out of me as I came undone on his cock.

"Little pain slut," Law whispered in my ear. "You fucking love this, don't you, babygirl?"

"Yes," I moaned despite myself. "Yes, Daddy!"

"Jesus," he bit out, fucking me so deep I rolled my eyes back. "That's right baby, you look so fucking good like this."

I let go, and only focused on his throbbing dick pounding inside me so fiercely every thrust made me cum. I stopped counting, stopped thinking. All of my orgasms rolled into one as he took what he wanted and gave me what I fucking needed.

"Lily," he muttered against my cheek, his thrusts getting harder. "What would mommy dearest think if she saw you now?"

He made me angry, and I wriggled under him, hissing curse words because I was still cumming and it felt so fucking wrong for him to be talking that way.

"What if mommy was only a floor above?" he taunted me, an evil smile on his fucking face. "What if I told you you've been in mommy's house all along, baby?"

I bit his shoulder, digging my teeth into his skin to stop myself from screaming when I came again. Law laughed at me, like I was fucking pathetic, but when my pussy tightened and swelled impossibly, his laughter turned into moans. He fucked me like he was a man possessed, pumping me so full I yelled his name, mixing it with Daddy.

I knew he was about to cum, my bruised and swollen pussy accommodating his huge size and squeezing tight to get what I really wanted. But when it happened, he just cursed out loud and his seed spilled inside me, hot and sticky and so fucking rewarding it just left me gasping for air.

He pulled out, grabbed me by the neck and made me look at his cock, slick and shiny with my juices and still throbbing. All I could think about was how it would taste in my mouth.

"See, babygirl," he grinned. "That's your virginity on my fucking cock. Now you're mine forever."

I came again, and I'd never been more ashamed of myself than in that moment.

CHAPTER 9

Law

I CLUTCHED AT THE COLLAR OF my white button-up shirt with one finger, trying to loosen it up without undoing the tie, at the same time balancing a glass of whiskey in that hand and a flute of champagne in the other. A part of me hoped that someone would walk straight into me, make me spill the drinks on my expensive suit, and get me the fuck out of there.

I had no such luck.

"Oh Lawson, honey, you're back," Emily called, waving at me as I made my way through the throng of bodies. "I thought you'd forgotten about me completely."

The titter of a laugh she let out scraped at my ears and I didn't reply to her, just handing over her drink and giving a slight nod to the people she was with. She wrapped an arm around my waist and snuggled in close, her silver, blinged out with Swarovski crystals dress making a gentle ruffling sound. I had to suppress the immediate urge to smack her for getting this fucking close to me.

Emily continued her conversation with the elderly couple across from us as we stood in the Raleigh Banquet Hall, attending the annual Concerned Mothers for Children's Safety benefit gala. The irony of the fact that they'd let someone like me, and someone like Emily, in here didn't escape me.

Everywhere I looked, I could see people wearing clothing and jewelry that screamed of wealth, rubbing elbows with other pricks just like them. It was like a who's who of the local aristocracy, and I'd never been in the company of people this fucking low. I mean, I'd been to some dark, bad places, but I could swear I'd never been exposed to this much callous disregard to human life anywhere else.

With criminals and the scum of the earth, you could at least usually understand why they were doing it. They were honest about it.

With rich people, though? The only reason they did

anything was because it would make them more profits. It didn't matter who they trampled over in the process.

"Don't you think so, Lawson?" Emily asked, batting her long lashes up at me.

"Hmm?"

I hadn't been paying attention to a single word she was saying.

"Oh, Emily, my dear, please excuse us. The Pendeltons have just arrived and we must say hello," the man we were evidently conversing with said, excusing himself and his wife.

"We'll do brunch, Emily," the woman said, sharing two quick kisses on the cheek with Emily.

It was like someone had untied an anchor from around my waist when Emily let go of me. I took a sip of the whiskey and it tasted more bitter than ever. It wasn't a good thing.

"They're such bores, aren't they?" Emily whispered, hiding her mouth behind her hand and adding in a girlish giggle. It made my skin crawl. "But Edward has always had a thing for pretty teenage boys, so who am I to question."

My mouth turned dry as I followed her through the crowd as she prompted me to, feeling like her very own trained lap dog. This was part of our deal. I was supposed to play the model husband, accompany her to her functions and make the questions go away.

"Oh Emily, when will you ever marry again after your dear Thomas!?"

I still remembered the first time she talked about her first husband, mimicking the way the women in her social circles asked her about her long lost 'better half'. The way she rolled her eyes at their naiveté had made my blood run cold, and I'd barely even known her then.

The band was playing something dull and slow and people were starting to head to the dance floor. Emily at least was wise enough not to even try and suggest that. There wasn't enough whiskey in the damn building to make me pretend like I wanted to hold her close to me when all I could really think about was my sweet little Lily, all alone back at the house.

"Are we about done here, Emily?" I asked her in a lowered voice as she came to a stop in the middle of the banquet hall, clearly looking for someone.

"No," she snapped at me shortly, not giving me even half a glance.

A growl rumbled in my chest but I silenced it. At home, being a haughty little bitch like that would have earned her a quick smack, but out here, she knew I couldn't touch her. Reminded me of someone else I know, playing the situation for her benefit...

"Oh, there they are," Emily said with a relieved sigh, pointing out a tall, broad-shouldered, middle-aged man and a petite, Asian-American woman out to me at the other end of the room.

I didn't need to ask who they were. Julie and Kent Ronson. The reason why we had to come to this shindig of human filth.

"Julie! Kent!" Emily greeted as we made our way over to them, with Emily sharing a lingering hug with Julie.

I shook hands with Kent as we introduced ourselves to one another. He had a firm handshake. It didn't surprise me. It didn't take much for one wolf to recognize another, though I doubted our methods were anything alike.

Julie looked at Emily as if she was seeing a vision, like the best thing that had ever happened to her had just walked up to her. I had to clear my throat to keep from chuckling. Poor little Julie. She had no idea what she had gotten herself into.

Emily seemed to forget all about Julie, who sidled back up to her husband as Emily's attention snapped to Kent.

"I'm so glad to see both of you here! It's been such a

bore, hasn't it, honey?" she asked, throwing a fleeting look my way.

I nodded curtly.

"It's about what you'd expect from these events, isn't it?" Kent commented, his words coming out in a slow, tortured drawl.

"I think they've done well with the decorations," Julie chimed in.

I could feel myself spacing out, having fulfilled my role of resident chaperone. I motioned to a passing waiter to get me a refill on my whiskey and as he sped off to go get it for me, it felt like the only immediate ray of hope I had to look forward to.

I was itching to ditch this place and go back to my babygirl. My cock throbbed in my pants as I thought of her, the image of her spread out for me, begging for my cock coming to my mind way too fucking easily.

So eager, so innocent, so ready... And all mine.

Emily's high-pitched laughter shook me out of my thoughts for a moment. I had to join in on the laughter, not knowing what we were laughing about, but sure I wouldn't have found it funny at the best of times. Sometimes, it still stunned me to know the lengths Emily would go to just to get her way.

The day I'd found Lily's picture looking back at me

on that website, I'd wondered who'd put a gorgeous little creature like her up for auction. It was a virgin auction site, the seediest of them all, and girls like Lily didn't end up in places like that.

They were sold at private auctions, attended by people like Kent and Edward, to be seen in flesh and poked and prodded before their new owners would decide to shell out what amounted to pocket change for the lives of innocent young women. I knew then that I couldn't afford her... and that I had to have her.

Tracking down who put her up on the site hadn't been too hard. Fuchsia, the call name of the person who had submitted her information, was an old pro in the business, having bought and sold virgins for at least a decade, if not more. I'd been expecting a chain-smoking aged reprobate behind a floral name like that.

Instead, I'd found Emily.

She'd gleefully explained to me how she'd put up Lily's information to find the right kind of buyer. Not the richest buyer, not the best buyer, but the right buyer. Someone who would be willing to negotiate, who could keep secrets... who had no morals.

Lo and behold, that man was me.

The fact that she was selling her own daughter didn't apparently change a fucking thing for Emily.

It had been years since I'd considered getting a girl for myself. The last time I got attached to someone was still too painful of a memory, but I knew I had to have Lily. After meeting her mother, that conviction only grew stronger. I knew that if I didn't get her, the guy Emily would find for her would ruin everything good about my little babygirl and only leave the bad.

Only leave the parts that had to have come from her bitch of a mother. The parts I was determined to get rid of.

I couldn't afford her then, not with money, which was what Emily had been banking on. So we made a different arrangement and there I was now, stuck in a sea of penguins, pretending like I belonged.

Since marrying Emily, things had changed. Knowing that Lily would eventually be mine, I'd built a legitimate business, needing to pour my energy into something while I waited for her. Construction was an easy enough business to crack, run mostly by people whose motivations I understood. My bank account was fat as fuck, but it had only been a distraction until I could get my hands on Lily.

Now that I had her, nothing really mattered. Least of all Emily, whose roof we were still living under. A predicament I'd have to see about fixing... As soon as Lily was well and truly broken in.

My mind drifted happily to all the ways I'd teach my

babygirl to behave, how I could take care of her and love her like no one else ever had or would. My drink arrived just in time and I swapped my empty glass for a full one, taking a long swig and letting it burn down my throat.

Every now and then, I'd have to nod or agree with Emily as we 'conversed' with the Ronsons, but thankfully no one expected me to be an active part of that conversation. I didn't need that kind of bullshit. I knew why we were here—so Emily could make an appearance with the right kind of people, including Kent, and Julie as a mandatory side-dish—and all I could do was to suffer through it.

The end of the night couldn't come soon enough. I needed to get back to my Lily.

Now that I'd had her tight pussy, being away from her felt like the definition of insanity. And I had plenty of that without any fucking help.

CHAPTER 10

Lily

THE MEMORIES OF HIM TAKING my virginity were still fresh in my mind, and my pussy ached pleasantly as I drifted off to sleep. I slid two fingers between my legs and felt the swollen lips of my cunt.

When Lawson came to me that night, it was definitely late. I'd been sleeping, wrapped up in the blanket he'd let me have the last time he was down in the cellar.

I woke up when someone lay on the mattress with me, my body tightening and going rigid with fear when another body joined mine.

"Shhh, babygirl, it's okay," a warm, rough voice

muttered into my ear, and I relaxed into Law's arms.

He'd never slept down here with me before, and he hadn't used the mattress unless he was fucking me. I could smell alcohol on his breath as he held me close. Not unpleasant, but definitely there.

A sudden urge to be closer to him prompted me to crawl into his arms and my lips found his in the darkness of the cellar. I kissed him softly, my lips molding against his and parting gently as an invitation. Lawson laughed and it made me reconsider what I was doing.

"You kiss like you're still a virgin," he groaned against my mouth.

He took my face in his hands and kissed me raw and deep, strong, capable arms pulling me on top of him. I obliged, swinging my legs over his body until I was straddling him.

"Is your little pussy still wet?" he muttered against my tits, and I arched my back in response. "I bet it is, babygirl."

To make sure he was right, he slipped a finger between my legs, finding me so wet it was embarrassing. It made him chuckle, and he brought his hand back to his lips and gave his fingers a long lick.

I hadn't stopped thinking about what we'd done the last time he was here with me for a second.

"I'll never get tired of the taste of you, baby," he told me gently, sucking his fingers dry from my juices.

It made me moan, and I rubbed my pussy on his pants, needy for more. Law settled his hands on my hips, and when he looked into my eyes, it felt like he was staring into my soul. I couldn't look away, my eyes trained on his as I moved my hips across his lap gently, like I was just playing a game with him.

"You're a little tease tonight," Law told me in a low voice, and I leaned down, my hair falling around us like a curtain shielding us from the outside world.

I kissed him again, pressing my naked tits and cunt against his clothes and breathing soft, moaning breaths into his mouth. His fingers dug into my sides and he groaned. I could feel him growing harder, throbbing with need, right under my pussy lips.

I remembered how his cock had entered me the day before, hard and cruel and oh so delicious. I licked his lips.

"Are you going to spend the night with me?"

The question slipped from my lips before I could stop it. I didn't like how needy I sounded. I needed to get a grip on myself.

He groaned and gently slid me off his lap, saying, "I can't, babygirl. I need to sleep upstairs."

"Why?"

I was aware of the whiny tone in my voice, and I think Law was, too. He unbuttoned his shirt and got up from the mattress, turning on the lamp that hung above us. I could see then that he was wearing dress clothes, like he'd just been out at an event or something. The knowledge bothered me, and knowing he had a life outside of this cellar, unlike me, upset me.

I shrank into the corner, crossing my arms in front of my body pointedly, but he didn't even look at me as he stumbled across the room. He bumped into the chair and cursed out loud.

"Are you okay?" I asked, too worried about him to remember my anger. "Did you have too much to drink?"

"I'm fine," he replied roughly, making me shrink back.

Law looked at me over his shoulder and sighed, running his fingers through his dark brown hair, which was slicked back that day.

"I'm sorry, sweetheart," he told me. "Just been a long day, is all. Daddy's feeling a little stressed."

I sat on my knees on the mattress, in a perfect position for him to take advantage of me. I was naked, and my nipples were getting hard under his watchful gaze.

"Can I do anything," I started. "To make Daddy feel better?"

Who was I and when had I become this? But I couldn't have stopped myself if I tried.

He gave me an affectionate smile, coming over to smooth my hair. His fingers lingered on my lips, and he grabbed my neck thoughtfully a moment later, lazily tightening his fingers around my throat.

"Such an obedient little girl," he muttered, then leaned down and kissed me one more time.

When he got up, the keys I'd seen last time were on the floor.

I gave him a panicked look, but Law didn't seem to notice. My heart was pounding so loudly I was sure he could hear it, but he merely turned around and turned off the light in the room.

"Get back to sleep, babygirl," he told me softly. "I'll see you tomorrow. We should both get some rest, it's been a long fucking day."

I lay back in the bed like I was on autopilot. The memory of the keys on the floor haunted me as Law left up the stairs and out of the room. He lingered in the doorway and I wondered whether he remembered his keys, but in the next second, he closed the door and the lock clicked into place. I figured the door locked itself when you closed it.

I lay there with my heart pounding for the next hour. I

couldn't even move, my body frozen up with fear and my mind wondering what I should do with Lawson's forgotten keys.

If I really were the good girl he thought I was, I would've saved them for the next time he came downstairs, giving them to him along with my free will.

But something awoke inside of me as I lay on that mattress. I couldn't give up just like that, could I?

Here was my chance to escape. Wasn't that what I'd been waiting for?

My hands shook badly as I reached for the keys, feeling the cold metal of them between my fingertips. I got off the mattress and walked toward the exit on shaky legs, my whole body trembling. And then I stopped abruptly.

What if this was all a test?

What if Law just wanted to see if I would try to escape, given the chance? What if I was going to get punished for this?

I already knew I would, if I didn't manage to get away. I knew he'd hurt me badly for trying to leave him. So I had to make it work, I had to run as fast as I could, move as quietly as possible, and get the fuck out of there.

In a haze, I put the key in the door and prayed it would unlock from the inside.

It did.

The door swung open and I stared at the stairs in front of me, unable to comprehend my freedom.

I was completely naked, and the stairs in front of me were dark and scary. I never thought escaping a madman would be this hard.

I half-crawled, half-walked up the stairs, my body shaking as I got to the top. A simple wooden door separated me from the outside world, from the confines of my prison. My hand shook as I reached for the knob and turned it to open the door.

Light engulfed me as I swung the door open. I looked around, bewildered as hell as my eyes adjusted to the brilliant light.

A kitchen, white marble and light wood, beautiful in its simplicity. No one had ever cooked here, with pristine pots and pans hanging above the counter and a bowl of untouched fruit sitting front and center on the bar.

I knew this kitchen.

A low, strangled cry ripped itself from my lips the moment my eyes connected with the woman standing at the counter, pouring herself a drink.

"Mommy?" I asked in a shaky voice.

She finished pouring herself the drink, not even giving me a glance. She put away the bottle while I shook in the doorway of the prison, and drank down the amber liquid while giving me a thoughtful look. She set down the glass on the marble counter with a clank and sighed.

"What are you doing, stupid girl?"

I tried walking up to her, forgetting about my nakedness as I stumbled into her arms. I started sobbing then, really fucking sobbing, low and desperate noises escaping me as I wet my mother's expensive dress with my tears.

She stood, unmoving, as I ruined her outfit. She didn't even put a hand on my exposed back to comfort me.

"Lily," she told me coolly. "Get the fuck back down there."

I moved away from her, sniffling and giving her a confused look through the tears clouding my vision.

"W-what?"

"Into the cellar," she repeated slowly.

I just stared at her, unable to understand what this meant, and she laughed gently, smoothing my hair down.

"Silly girl," she said. "You haven't learned anything, have you?"

I bit back a sob as she advanced on me. I felt like I was being hunted, and the only way to escape was to retreat back. I took a step away from her, back toward my prison.

"You like him, don't you?" my mother asked me pointedly. "You have it good, girl. It could be so much worse, I hope you know that. He's good to you, and you're falling for him."

I shook my head wildly and she merely laughed, an awful, throaty sound.

"Don't lie to yourself, Lily."

I took another step back as she advanced on me, feeling myself standing in the doorway that lead down into the cellar.

"Just stop being such a fucking brat."

Her attitude changed, and she was pissed now, spitting the words at me.

"Get the fuck back down there."

I didn't move, and she took another angry step forward, almost making me stumble.

"Now, Lily."

I was frozen to the spot.

She sighed and with the flick of her fingers, she pushed me down the stairs.

It felt like I was still falling when I dropped at the bottom of the stairs like a stone. I looked up, my body bruised and hurting as my mother stood at the top of the stairs, illuminated by the light of the kitchen no one in our family ever used.

"Be a good girl, Lily," she told me, and she slammed the door shut.

This time I heard another lock clicking into place, and I crawled into a corner of the stairwell, curling up into a little ball.

There were no tears this time, only memories.

I remembered my father, how good he was to me and how my mother had always accused me of being a daddy's girl. I remembered how he'd stood up for me when mom was being especially vicious, how he'd defended me from her any chance he got.

But there was no daddy to stand up for me now—I was on my own. And as hard as I'd tried to escape my mother, it seemed like she was still the one in charge. Now, during the darkest time of my life, a part of me wasn't even surprised to find out that she had something to do with it.

Another memory surged to the surface.

An image of my father, tired and sick, as he descended a flight of stairs from our family kitchen.

I'd never had that memory before, and my eyes widened as it crystallized in my mind then and there. It made my heart pound with fear, and the image kept replaying itself in my mind over and over again. Dad going down the stairs, throwing one last look, one last smile at me over his shoulder.

"Daddy," I cried out, even though I knew no one would hear me, no one would fucking care. "Help me, please."

That was when the tears really started to come.

CHAPTER 11

Law

THE CANE FELT HEAVY IN my hand as I unlocked the door, finding Lily curled up on the mattress.

"Stand up, Lily," I told her, letting the door slowly fall shut behind me.

The keys were back in my pocket. Emily had held onto them for the night, waiting until the next morning to tell me what had happened between her and her daughter. The thought of Lily having to go through that alone twisted me up inside, but I couldn't focus on that.

She'd tried to leave me.

Lily didn't move, lying naked and quiet as a mouse, her

nose against the wall. She wasn't crying, but her breath was coming in quick heaves. My heart broke, knowing that she'd probably been in a mire of her own twisted thoughts the whole night and I hadn't been here to help her.

But she'd tried to fucking leave me.

"Lily, I told you to do something."

That made her stir. She looked at me, her eyes red with tears. I was sure she hadn't slept a wink.

I waited patiently, weighing the cane in my hands. Finally, she gathered herself off the floor and stood, facing me. Her shoulders were slumped and her face ashen, having nothing to do with the dim lighting in the cellar.

My head was still throbbing slightly from one too many whiskeys the night before—it had been all I could do to keep from socking Kent in his smug, arrogant face, knowing what he did to get off on his free time—but one good look at her could always clear that up. This time, though, there was a lump in the bottom of my stomach, weighing there heavily.

She wanted to leave me.

"Turn around. Hands against the wall."

"Daddy," she whispered, eyes glistening.

"No," I stopped her before she could keep going. "Hands against the wall. Now."

Quietly, letting her head drop, she relented and turned around, putting her hands against the cool wall. I stepped behind her, lingering there for a moment, breathing in her scent, before I spread her legs with my booted foot. I was in jeans and a ragged tee that morning, wearing combat boots and looking as far as I could have from my last night's carefully groomed self. I finally felt like my fucking self again.

"You were a bad girl for Daddy," I started quietly, running the tip of the cane up from behind her right knee until it was poking into her firm buttocks, making a dimple there. "You shouldn't have done that, Lily. I'm very disappointed."

She nodded wordlessly and I saw her chest heave in a soundless sob. Good. She had to feel bad. She had to understand that she could never leave me.

Everything I did was to ensure that she could never get away, never go back to the world that would eat her up and spit her out. Never be alone again, faced with things that she couldn't handle.

That's why she had to be here. That's why she had to be here with me.

So I could keep her safe.

"I can't protect you if you're not by Daddy's side," I told her lazily, running the cane up her back now, and

DADDY'S GIRL | 115

then down her spine until it reached between her ass cheeks, the hard, solid wood spreading the plump globes in a way that made my cock twitch. "You can't run away from me, Lily."

The words came out more forceful than I had intended them. I felt a pounding in my chest, spreading through my whole body when I thought of what could have happened had she gotten away. Or if Emily had decided to make use of the situation and sell her off to another bidder under the guise of her escaping.

The months of waiting to get my babygirl with me had been torture, imagining her out in the world all on her own with no one to keep her safe. Now, my worst nightmare had almost come true while I was fucking passed out in the other room. My grip tightened around the cane.

"Tell me you understand."

"Yes, Daddy," she said, the fight gone from her voice.

I didn't like that. She went through spells of being good for me, but I liked the fire in her, the bratty side of her. It felt like Emily had done a fine fucking job of taking it out of her last night.

"Good," I said, rubbing the cane lower now, spreading her pussy with it.

I yanked the cane upward and she gasped, having to

rise to her tiptoes as the wood bore between her sweet lips. I loved the little yelp she made. Pulling back the cane, I shoved my fingers roughly between her legs, making her wince and her knees almost buckle as I fingered her cunt. She was dry. That couldn't stand.

"You need to be punished now, babygirl," I whispered in her ear, wanting to press myself against her but keeping back.

She couldn't know how fucking hard it was making me, seeing her ride that cane, even though I still wanted to shake her for being so fucking stupid and trying to run away.

Didn't she realize she wouldn't be happy without me?

This is going to hurt me as much as it's going to hurt you, Lily, I thought, taking a step back and swinging the cane in my hand.

"You need to count out every hit and ask for one more, babygirl," I told her, and she nodded like a good girl.

I didn't give her a chance to take a breath before the first hit of the wooden cane smacked against her pure, pretty ass. The welts from the belt were gone, but I'd make sure there would be new ones. Her whole body shook as she flattened herself against the wall, her knees clanking into it as she nearly collapsed. The wail came a second later, stuck in her chest before.

"Count it," I demanded, the hit reverberating through me like someone had just caned me over the back.

"One!" she squealed through tears, her forehead against the wall. "One more, please, Daddy!"

"Good girl," I said, hitting her again at the same time.

She buckled again, picking herself up quicker this time though, and the scream came without holding back.

"Count it," I hissed, my arm feeling like it was going to fall off from having to punish her like this.

"Two," she whined. "One more, please, Daddy!"

The next one was aimed a little lower, almost grazing her thighs but not quite. She counted without me having to tell her this time, her nails scratching at the wall in agony.

I told myself that I had to do this. For her sake. For both our sakes. If she got away... I couldn't live with myself.

The next time I caned her, she glanced at me over her shoulder, and her blue eyes were brimming with tears, more already falling down her cheeks. She kept eye contact as she mouthed the words, almost unintelligible between the sobs of pain.

She looked so much like Chloe that time that it almost made me stop.

I shook my head.

"Face the wall, Lily," I told her, hitting her again as soon as she did.

Visions of Chloe swam in my head, bitter memories filing in right after them. She'd been a good girl... not nearly as difficult as Lily. She learned fast, broke fast, and was built up even faster. But she was never mine.

Just another girl I was breaking in for someone else, doing the job they paid me to do. Back then, it had been fine. I had my fun, I could make sure that the girl was taught proper manners before getting to her new Master, and I was paid handsomely for it.

Chloe had been the one to change it all for me.

I counted the hits in my head as I caned Lily. The seventh one smacked across her ass still, red and blotchy now.

"Eight," she whimpered.

Before she could say the next one, I hit her across her lower thighs. The scream that bellowed out of her chest was so loud it felt like it was shaking the foundation of the house.

"That was eight. No fucking cheating."

"Eight! Please one more, Daddy," she said, stumbling over the words.

So I gave her what she asked for.

Her body looked like it was being held up by the wall as she clung to it desperately, her nails scrabbling across the concrete. Her pale body was shaking, frail and bare and for me to do as I pleased. I wondered if she'd ever try to run again after I was done with her.

Chloe had never tried to run. She'd eaten up every word and taken every punishment, reveling in it with just the right mix of pleasure and horror. The day I had to let her go to her new Master, I almost didn't do it.

I didn't want to do it. But it was my job.

A week later, Chloe was dead.

Her new prick of a Master didn't have the faintest idea about safety. He ended up choking her to death during one of their sessions. After that, I hadn't taken another job. I hadn't taken another girl.

Until Lily.

"Fifteen," she all but whispered. "Please, one more, Daddy!"

"Good girl," I murmured, leaning closer to her.

I dropped my head between her shoulder blades, feeling her body jump as I smacked her right thigh this time. I stayed there, the hits getting more localized, shorter, sharper, until she counted twenty and I let the cane drop from my hand.

Wrapping one arm around her waist, I caught her right before she was about to collapse on her knees. Carefully, I slid my other hand between her legs, over her throbbing ass, and felt her pussy.

The chuckle that crossed my lips was dark and humorless. She was soaking wet for me.

"My little pain slut," I whispered.

She made a noise but didn't say a word as I hauled her up and carried her to the corner furthest from her mattress. There, I put her down, letting her fall on her knees. Her legs couldn't hold her up anymore, the adrenaline slowly wearing off.

Leaving her there, I made the chain of the leg clasp shorter and then snapped it around her ankle again. She couldn't make it to the mattress, or the bathroom, and she definitely couldn't fucking run.

I crouched down behind her, her head propped on the wall again.

"You're going to stay here, just like this, until Daddy comes back. You won't move an inch. You will think about what you did and you will never try to fucking run again. Is that understood, Lily?" I asked her sternly.

"Yes, Daddy," came the immediate answer.

I'd never wanted to fuck her more than I did at that

moment. So I got up, walked out of the room, and made sure the keys were still in my pocket.

I wasn't going to repeat my mistakes. No one was going to hurt Lily but me, least of all her mother.

CHAPTER 12

Lily

B Y THE TIME I HEARD the lock turning again, I was so far gone I was convinced it was my imagination playing tricks on me.

But no—a moment later I saw Lawson's handsome face before mine as he crouched in front of me, slumped in the corner of the dingy room.

"Hello, babygirl," he said sweetly.

His hand reached for me and I whimpered when the rough skin on his fingers made contact with my soft cheek. I leaned against him, drained and tired and most of all, deeply embarrassed because of everything that had happened.

"Did my little girl learn her lesson?" Law asked me, and I nodded so fast it made me hiccup. He grinned at me, a chuckle escaping his lips as he slowly undid the chain around my ankle. He helped me up by offering me his hand, but the moment I tried to get to my feet, my knees gave way and I tumbled to the floor.

Law tsk-ed at me and grabbed my waist, helping me to my feet again and guiding me toward the small bathroom in the cellar.

"Keep your strength, baby," he told me. "You're gonna need a lot more if you want to stick around."

He put me down on the toilet, and this time I didn't even have the energy to argue. I had to pee so bad I just let it go, sniffling pathetically as I emptied my bladder.

Law hummed to himself as I finished up, then helped me off the toilet. He flushed it for me and washed my hands, his rough fingers surprisingly gentle when he lathered mine with soap and washed it all off.

I was still naked, and even though it wasn't particularly cold in the cellar, I was shivering like crazy as Law led me back inside the room.

"I brought some toys for us to play with today," Law told me, pointing toward a bag I hadn't noticed earlier. It was a big leather hold-all, and my skin prickled with unwanted excitement as I tried to imagine what was in there.

"You want to play with Daddy, sweetheart?" Law asked me softly as I sat on the mattress. I was quick to nod, scooting closer to him where he stood and hugging his knees.

"Use your words, babygirl," Law reminded me sternly, and I looked up at him with my eyes brimming with tears for no apparent reason.

I was so happy he was back.

"I want to play, Daddy," I managed to get out, and he gave me a grin as he petted my head. Then, he left me on the floor and retrieved the leather bag, placing it at my feet and motioning for me to open it.

The whole time he was away, the worst thing about waiting for him wasn't the fact that I had to stay where I was told, but because a part of me was panicking that he wouldn't come back at all.

"Go on," he encouraged me. "It's not going to bite, sweetheart."

I bit my bottom lip before digging into the bag. The first thing I noticed at the top were some warm towels and a big tub of some kind of ointment. Law took it from my hand and unscrewed the top.

"Lie on your tummy," he told me, and I obeyed.

Images of him caning me were fucking with my mind, but I pushed them into the farthest corner of my mind and focused on a happier place. I felt something cool being smoothed into the welts on my ass, and I hissed when Law's hand rubbed the pain all over my butt.

"Shhh, babygirl," he cooed. "I'm only going to make it better, don't worry."

And he was right. As he massaged the cream into my hurt ass, I could feel the ointment getting hotter on my skin, seeping into the welts he'd put there. He smoothed his fingers over every inch of me, until every welt felt like it was on fire. It was weird, but I liked it.

"What is that?" I asked him over my shoulder, my eyes almost fearful as they connected with his. "What did you put on me?"

"It's some old Asian remedy," Law explained. "It'll make you feel better. And it has different uses."

I should've known what his wicked grin meant as he ordered me to lie on my ass.

I winced when the welts touched the mattress. I lay still as I possibly could, completely exposed to Law's hungry eyes. He reached for the tub again and crouched next to me, his fingers going inside the pot and coming back white with the cream he'd used on my back.

"Spread your pussy for Daddy, baby," he told me gently.

With shaky fingers, I reached between my legs and parted myself for him, opening up like a flower under his eyes.

"Good little slut," Law told me. His voice and movements were gentle as he reached forward and his fingertips connected with my exposed pussy.

It felt cool and pleasant at first but as soon as Law moved away, I could feel it—the slow, steady burn of the cream against my folds and clit.

"It burns," I told him in a shaky voice. "Please, Daddy, it feels really hot."

"Good," he told me as he put the tub of cream aside. "It'll make you nice and wet for when Daddy's ready for your cunt."

I pulled my legs up and he didn't stop me. He was digging in the bag when I curled up, snuggling up to his leg.

"I'm sorry I ran," I whispered against his leg. I was hungry and exhausted, tired from barely any sleep, but I wanted more than anything for him to forgive me.

I'd been so fucking stupid.

Trapped right under my mother's house, so close to her and yet in a completely different world. I'd never had a great relationship with my mother, but I think my brain still couldn't quite comprehend what she had been willing to do to me.

This man had forced me into the dark, grim cellar, and for reasons I couldn't understand, he was still the only thing I wanted right then.

"I know I deserved the punishment," I muttered into his jeans, and then looked up into Law's eyes. "I'm glad it's all over now."

His expression was unreadable as he said, "It's not over, babygirl. That was just the first part. Now be quiet."

I paled but knew better than to argue. The cream was really starting to burn now, and along with the heat spreading from my pussy I felt this overwhelming desire to cum.

I sneaked a hand between my legs the moment Law came back to stand beside me.

"Hands fucking off," he told me roughly. "Or am I going to have to tie you up so you don't touch yourself like a naughty little slut?"

"No, Daddy." My mouth was dry as I removed my hand, rubbing myself helplessly against the mattress. It was crazy, I was so wet and horny, so needy for any kind of friction I would've done anything to get myself off.

He crouched next to me again and I gave him a desperate look that made him chuckle.

"I brought you a gift," he told me. "I hear pretty girls like you like jewelry."

My eyes widened, and he brought out a hand from behind his back. There was a weird object in it, something made of glass with a crystal bead on one end. As I realized what it was, my eyes watered and I cried out his name.

"Shhh, baby," he cooed. "It's Daddy here, remember? I could hurt you for that, but you're so pretty when you cry I might not. Now get on your knees."

I did as I was told, my pussy so on fire I bucked my hips as I got into position. I felt Law behind me, forcing my legs wider apart. My knees were sore from the endless kneeling I'd done, waiting for him to get back. I should have known I would only get on my knees again as soon as he was here.

"Hold your ass," he told me in a low voice. "Hold your ass open for Daddy."

I choked on a needy little sob and did it. I gasped when I felt my tiny asshole widen for him, and then something wet sliding down my back, cruel fingers spreading the wetness from my pussy up to my ass and making it drip. I realized with a start he'd spit on me .

I felt like I was on fire, so needy I saw white before my eyes.

"Are you ready, babygirl?" he asked me sweetly. "Ready for your pretty plug?"

I whimpered and he smacked my ass, making me jump.

"Words, Lily," he reminded me sternly. "Use your fucking words."

"Y-yes," I stuttered. "Daddy, please. I want it inside me, please..."

I felt something pushing inside me, stretching me impossibly and making me cry out like a fucking animal. The plug stretched me wide and I gasped like I was dying as he filled my ass with it. And then it was in, and it was as if the stretching sensation never ended, my ass gaping around the plug he'd pushed inside me and holding me wide open.

"Hold it in with your hand," Law ordered me. "Your ass is too tight, baby, it won't stay in otherwise."

I obeyed with shaky fingers, moaning as I pushed the plug deeper inside my body. Law moved away from me and I looked up at him, pathetic tears running down my cheeks because this wasn't nearly enough to get me off, my pussy screaming for attention between my shaking thighs.

"You're so fucking beautiful," Law muttered to himself. "Jesus, Lily."

He unzipped his pants excruciatingly slowly and brought out his cock. I whimpered at the sight of it, trying desperately to get him to fuck me as he started to play with it. He pumped his fist over his length, fast and hard and greedy, as he looked at me.

I shut my eyes tightly, feeling the hotness spreading from my pussy throughout my whole body. It was insane, and the sensations of having my ass filled completed with my pussy burning up was almost too much too take. I was constantly on the verge of cumming, but nothing fucking pushed me over the edge.

By the time I managed to open my eyes again, Law's cock was throbbing so hard the tip was almost purple. He let out a guttural growl and moved toward me.

The moment he pushed his throbbing, veiny cock inside my dripping wetness felt like insanity, the relief so great I screamed for Daddy over and over again. I came the moment his cock was inside me, begging and cursing and pleading for more.

He didn't fuck me like a caring Daddy. He fucked me like a damn beast, claiming my pussy with every thrust of his powerful hips. I never stopped cumming, not even when his fingers joined mine to push the plug deeper. He reduced me to a whimpering, sobbing and pathetic little mess that only knew three words.

"Please, Daddy, more."

He leaked his cum inside my pussy and cursed when

he did. I knew he didn't mean to finish so fast but I felt oddly proud in my delirium at having made him cum like that. He pulled out of me and I felt the trickle of his cum down my pussy lips.

"Stay down," he ordered me roughly. "Ass up, face down, babygirl."

He moved away from me and I blinked the tears of pure bliss and pain away as he stood back to look at me. I was a mess, I was sure of it, and yet neither of us seemed to care.

"Jesus, you are beautiful," he muttered to himself, repeating what he'd said before. "Next time, I'm taking pictures."

Despite knowing that this was twisted and weird, I'd never felt so beautiful than when he said that.

His cock was still throbbing, still fucking hard, and I wasn't even sure whether I could take him looking at me like this, let alone touching me with those hands of his.

My lips parted and I begged, "Please, Daddy. More..."

CHAPTER 13

Law

"*L*AW, IS THAT YOU?" EMILY called as I stepped in through the front door, shrugging off my jacket.

I didn't respond. It had been a long day, checking up on some of the construction sites after neglecting them for weeks, and I was in no mood to deal with her bullshit. That being said, I was never in a mood for it, but that wasn't something I had much of a choice in currently.

Something to be fixed, I thought, walking through the house and making a beeline for the door leading to the cellar.

Lily had been acting strange since our little caning session and I was determined to find out what the fuck that was about. If it provided a way to circumvent whatever conversation Emily wanted to have, that'd be all the better.

"Lawson," she huffed, just as my hand was hovering over the door handle.

"What?" I asked, my tone betraying how on edge I was as I turned around to face her.

She was looking at me with an arched brow, her arms crossed over her chest. She was the perfect picture of high-class suburbanite condemnation, in her silk blouse and high heels. I couldn't imagine a woman less appealing at the moment.

"I just wanted to tell you that we'll be having a dinner soon. And I'll need Lily there, so you should prepare her to go out in public," Emily said coyly, tilting her head to the side. "I assume that won't be a problem?"

"Where the fuck do you want to take her?"

"Not her alone. Both of you. We're having a little soirée and I want you both to be there. Details to follow!"

She grinned at me and turned to leave, as if she'd told me something as common as what our dinner plans were going to be. I grabbed her by the shoulder and roughly spun her around to face me before she could get a step in.

Gasping, she pushed her hands against my chest, but I put distance between us as soon as she did that. I didn't want her hands on me.

The only hands that were supposed to be on me were Lily's.

"You're going to tell me what the hell you're planning, Emily," I ground out.

She tried to give me the look again, but I wasn't having any of it. Rolling her eyes, she sighed dramatically, reminding me too much of the Lily I'd seen posting her Facebook Lives all over her page. Full of herself, entirely certain the world owed her... but in Lily's case, I knew that was a front to hide insecurities.

With Emily, I was sure it was the real deal. What you saw was what you got.

"We're invited to a dinner. You, me, and Lily."

"How does anyone know she's even in town?" I asked, narrowing my eyes.

"I told them, of course," Emily said with a grin. "Don't be ridiculous! She's my daughter, my only child! Of course I want to show her off."

"She's not yours anymore," I said, feeling rage rising in me.

This was not good. Things were never fucking good

with Emily, but I knew for certain that she was planning something now. Something I wouldn't like, and that had very little to do with her motherly love for her daughter.

"She'll always be mine," Emily said coolly, her lips pressed into a thin line. "Haven't you had enough fun with her already? Aren't you getting bored yet? I can find you something new, something much more fun... Another virgin, maybe? Plenty of blue-eyed blondes with daddy issues running around... just your type."

My hands balled into fists at my sides and it took everything I had to keep from snapping her neck right then and there.

"I'll never be 'done' with her."

"You're going to have to be," Emily murmured, and I felt like the ground beneath my feet shifted slightly. "We're having dinner with Kent and Julie. And you'll both be there, or I swear I'll take her away from you so fast that the only thing you'll see is jail bars sliding into place in front of your face."

Emily sneered, clearly reading my reaction for what it was. My fists were balled up so tight my knuckles were turning white.

"You'll be on your best behavior, and she will be on her best behavior. You'll make sure of that. I know you will. It's your job, after all."

Emily turned to leave again, likely satisfied with her handiwork, when my hand reached out on its own volition and grabbed her thick mane of blonde hair. I pulled her back, making her fly against the nearest wall with her shoulder taking the brunt of the hit.

I didn't make a habit of hurting women like that, in fact I fucking despised it, but Emily wasn't even human-adjacent for me at that point. She was just... evil. And I knew evil.

Before she could slip away, I grabbed her bruised shoulder with one hand and pushed her against that wall again.

"You're going to do no such fucking thing," I told her, seething with anger.

"Try me, Lawson," she cooed, her flawless veneer of disinterest back in place though that shoulder had to hurt like hell. "You don't think I have contingencies in place for you acting like a fucking fool? You'll do as I say or you'll both pay, and I'll make sure that it's Lily who will be remembering it for the rest of her life."

We stared at one another, locked in our mutual dislike for one another. I'd always looked at her as a means to an ends and it was only now dawning on me how much both her daughter and our arrangement was the same for her. I don't know why, but I guess a part of me had still assumed she cared a little about her daughter...

Though handing her over to the likes of me probably went against that assumption on every level.

I knew one thing, though. I was a bad man, but I was nowhere near as bad as Kent Ronson could be. And there was no fucking way he was going to lay a hand on my babygirl.

I let Emily go reluctantly, taking a step back. She straightened herself, smoothing back her hair like she'd just been brushed by an annoying wisp of wind and nothing more. As much as I wanted to wring her neck, I had to believe her. Emily was exactly the kind of woman to have fallbacks in place for ensuring that she got what she wanted.

All I could do was to make sure that I could keep Lily as safe as possible. And that meant being around to protect her.

I went for the cellar door and pulled it open, passing through without a look Emily's way.

When the door fell shut behind me, I heard the last words she deemed necessary to share with me: "You didn't think you were going to get to keep her, did you?" followed by laughter.

CHAPTER 14

Law

I STOMPED DOWN THE STAIRS, SOUNDING like a platoon was storming the house, not just one man. Teeming with anger, it was all I could do not to go upstairs and finish what I started with Emily.

It took conscious effort to unclench my fisted hand. The muscles felt as if they had hardened into place, tight and sinewy, waiting to be unleashed on something or someone. When I came to the door leading into Lily's cell, I had to stop and breathe.

I must have stood there for ten minutes, my mind a red, angry blank, trying to bring myself down from that high of rage. When I unlocked the door, I felt like every breath out of me no longer came as steam and aggravation, but just barely.

"Lily, come here," I said, finding her sitting on the mattress, idly plaiting her hair.

She'd need a new shower soon. I'd made her filthy the last time I was here, and my cock twitched with the thought of having her wrapped around it again. But I couldn't take my anger out on her. I had intended to break her, but not like that.

Taking a seat on the lone chair in the room, I patted a spot on my thigh when she looked up at me, blue eyes showing her confusion.

"Did I do something wrong, Daddy?" she asked me, and it made my heart ache for a moment.

"No," I said, the word coming out gruffer than I intended. "I mean... no, you didn't. Come here, babygirl, get on my lap."

I practically sighed as I said that, motioning her forward. She perked up, showing me a slight smile as she scrambled up. She hesitated for a moment, like she was expecting me to tell her to get on her hands and knees and crawl. Any other time, I just might have.

She's learned well, I thought.

I didn't say anything, letting her figure out her

boundaries for herself. When she settled on being brave, she quickly crossed the scant few feet between us and gingerly sat down on my lap. I curled an arm around her waist and pulled her in tighter, grabbing her legs with the other and pulling them across my wide thighs as well.

I wanted to have her close, to feel like she couldn't be removed from me, damned how anyone tried.

Her scent was sweet, but it was different from how it had been the first time I'd breathed her in. It wasn't the conditions she was kept in or anything to do with that.

The air around her was different. Though she obviously had no space to make up her mind about her life like she used to when living alone away from her mother, it almost felt like she was more confident somehow. It was familiar, in a bittersweet way.

"Is your ass still in pain, Lily?" I asked her.

"No," she said, shaking her head. "Well, a little... but it's not bad."

She bit her lower lip and I chuckled, her eyes lighting up with a smile as well. I kept feeling like she was waiting for the other shoe to drop, but I couldn't be angry with her now. Her punishment had ended and ironically, mine felt like it was only about to begin.

"Are you telling me you want more?"

She shook her head, but it came out a little too slow,

 DADDY'S GIRL | 141

like she was thinking about it. I already knew she had a penchant for pain. Many of the girls I'd had had shared that trait. Maybe I was just good at bringing it out.

"Don't you lie to me, babygirl," I said sternly.

She looked down sharply, her fingers ceasing playing with the hem of my shirt for a moment.

"Maybe," she all but whispered.

I kissed her on the temple and chuckled.

"That's better."

We sat in silence for a while, the kind that I was loathe to break. It felt like the only time I was really in my head was when I was around her now, and every time I left the cell the world would do its fucking best to screw me, and by proxy her, over. Though truthfully the world could mostly be condensed down to mommy dearest at this point.

"Is everything alright, Daddy?"

I had to consider that. The only honest answer was no, but I couldn't really tell her that.

"It is what it is," I said with a shrug, hating the fact that I almost sounded resigned to it. "Is there anything I can do?"

I grinned. Looking at my little pet, thinking she could fix the problems I had created for us.

The fact that she dared, and wanted, to ask meant a lot to me, though. I brushed her hair back, the untied plait falling loose over her shoulder. My thumb lingered on her soft cheek, moving slowly to her lips, and I caught the way her breath hitched as she waited for me to keep going.

I was getting hard, like I always did around her, but this was not the time.

"Not this time, babygirl," I murmured.

She wasn't satisfied with that answer, her brow furrowing slightly.

"Maybe if you talk about it..." she started, trailing off.

I pulled a hand through my hair, considering my options here. On the one hand, she was my prisoner, my pet and my toy. On the other hand, her wicked witch of a mother was doing her best to make our combined future as uncertain as she could, and a part of me felt that Lily had the right to know.

"Have you understood how all of this happened?" I asked her.

She returned my gaze, dumbfounded, shaking her head. I guess she was as surprised that I was bringing this up as I was.

"Your mother sold you to me, Lily. Or to be exact, she traded you for my services."

"Your... services?" Lily asked, her face ashen now and the lovely pink blush of her cheeks that I'd come to enjoy so much completely gone now.

"Yes, my services," I confirmed. "I'm a bad man, Lily, and I think I don't have to explain this to you. I've been a bad man for a long time, but when I saw your picture, I knew I had to have you... and that you'd be my last one."

"Your last one?"

"The last girl I'd break in... the last woman I wanted," I told her candidly. "I couldn't afford to buy you outright, and I think your mother never intended to just trade you for money. She needed someone to do her bidding, someone to give her legitimacy as a... well, as a person, and as a businesswoman.

"I've done this for a living, taken pretty little things like you and made them ready for people worse than I am, for a long time. You mother's been selling people as sex slaves, Lily, but she's never managed to really break into the business. With me by her side, married to her, it gave her clout that she couldn't get any other way."

Lily listened to me, transfixed, shock and horror mixing with sadness on her face. It hadn't been lost on me that she and her mother had never had a real relationship, but Emily was still Lily's parent. Someone that was supposed to look out for her, or at the very least set an example as a person. Emily had failed at both, but I knew Lily had no idea how badly she'd done so.

"She gave you to me in exchange for me being with her and lending my name to her enterprise, but I don't think she's done selling you, babygirl."

My insides twisted when I said that. Lily's eyes brimmed with tears almost immediately and I grabbed her tight, pushing her head to my shoulder before the first strangled whimper escaped between her lips. I guess though she'd run into her mother during her failed escape attempt, the severity of Emily's betrayal hadn't sunk in yet.

Well, it had now, and I felt like the monster I was for letting this happen to her. But she needed to know the truth if worst came to worst and Emily managed to do something that I couldn't protect her from.

"W-why?" she asked through quiet sobs, looking up at me.

I shrugged my shoulders, feeling oddly defeated. If someone had told me a year ago that I'd let anyone have as much power over me as Emily did right now, I would have punched them in the fucking mouth. I guess it was poetic in a way, trapped by both the mother and the daughter, and in such completely opposite ways.

I kissed the top of her head now.

"That's what monsters do," I said. "They wreak havoc."

I wasn't sure whether I was talking about myself or Emily at this point. If the shoe fits...

"I need you to know that I'll do whatever I can to make sure that we stay together. That she doesn't do a thing to you."

Lily nodded tentatively, and I smiled.

"That's a good girl. I'll bring you some nicer things soon. I think you deserve them."

That got a small smile out of her, but I knew it wasn't because I'd promised her something nice. It was just because I was showing her a bit of kindness, a grace that I hadn't revealed to her until now. All I wanted was to make her feel good, the focus in my head having sharply shifted from my personal satisfaction to hers.

"Thank you, Daddy," she said with a sigh, wiping tears from her cheek as she collapsed against my shoulder again.

I rubbed her arms, keeping her close. I never wanted to leave this cell. It had never felt like a prison to me, though it must have to her. For me, it was more of a sanctuary than anything else.

Somewhere to hide away from the fucking mess I'd created. But that couldn't last. I had to get in control of this before it went too far, and I didn't have a lot of time with which to do it.

CHAPTER 15

Lily

"*L*ILY?"

I looked up, rubbing the sleep from my eyes to the voice calling my name. My lips parted in slight shock when I saw my mother standing at the door leading into the cellar. The corners of her lips were up-turned in a grotesque smile and her distaste for this room was obvious.

For a moment, I was sure I was dreaming.

"Lily, come here," my mother called out again.

"Mom?" I picked myself up from the mattress and ran a hand through my ratty hair. "What are you doing here?"

She gave me a tight-lipped smile and motioned for me to come toward her. Countless occasions of feeling like I was being dissected by her judgmental gaze ran through my head, but I pushed them aside.

My heart beat with newfound hope and I rushed into her arms, forgetting about the fact that I was stark naked, something I'd usually try to cover up. Law had undone the chain the night before and I was now free to roam the room as I saw fit.

Before I reached and embraced her, mom made me stop with a single motion of her outstretched hand.

"No, darling, please," she said stiffly. "You look dirty."

I stood there like a lost puppy, self-consciously covering my dirty body from her critical gaze. Finally, she turned around and started walking out of the room.

"Come with me, Lily."

I almost couldn't believe her words. She wanted me to follow her outside, just like that? I was sure this was some kind of test Law had made her do.

I stood in the cellar, unmoving, and staring at her retreating back. When she finally noticed I wasn't coming, she turned around and gave me a stern look.

"Lily, don't make me drag you out of there," she told me roughly.

"I... I don't want to break any rules," I stumbled over the words. "Daddy—... I mean Law said I'm not supposed to run."

"You're not running, stupid girl," my mom sneered at me. "You're leaving with me because I told you to do so, and my word is the law down here, not his."

She chuckled at her own pun, but motioned for me to follow her again in the next second. My heart was pounding as I took a step closer to the door, but when the time came for me to step out of the cellar, I couldn't bring myself to do it. I just stood there, completely frozen and unable to take another step that could lead me to my freedom.

"Lily," mom called out. "Are you coming?"

"Please," I said softly. "I don't want to upset him. He told me not to try and leave."

"Upset him?" Mom stormed back down the stairs and grabbed ahold of my hair, pulling on my mane so hard she made me cry out in pain. "You're going to do as I say, girl. I'm the one you should be listening to here, not your stepdaddy."

"Oh, Lily," my mom smiled like I was some pathetic, helpless little creature. Like she felt really fucking sorry for me. "You still don't know shit, do you?"

She dragged me up the stairs by my hair, and when we reached the kitchen, I stopped fighting. It hurt too much, the pull on my hair so hard it was tearing my hair out in chunks.

"We're getting you washed up," mom told me roughly. "I wish you'd been a good girl, Lily, and we didn't have to do this the hard way."

She pushed me into the downstairs bathroom, one I'd used so many times before. I looked at it with different eyes today, big and wide as I took in the luxuries I didn't even bother to think about earlier.

Towels, soft and fluffy. Soap, flower scented and creamy in color.

The room was cleaner than I had been in weeks.

Mom forced me into the bathtub and I hugged my knees to my chest, sitting down. Everything that Law had told me was making me see my mother in a different light now.

She turned on the shower and I screeched when the freezing water hit my dirty skin.

"That's what you get for being a damn brat," mom told me sternly, and pointed the showerhead in my face.

I started crying, the hot tears almost a relief compared to the ice-cold water that she was spraying me with. My skin erupted in goosebumps as she washed me like it was a chore, her hands rough when she tugged and pulled on my hair.

"Maniac," she muttered to herself. "Couldn't even bring you a damn brush to get these knots out."

Despite everything that had happened, I found myself leaning against her, looking for comfort my mother had never been able to give me. I let her tear through my hair while the icy water pounded my skin, until she moved back and sighed dramatically.

"I can't get through that damn mess," she complained. "We're going to have to cut it."

"W-what?" I stuttered, giving her a look through eyelashes wet with tears. "Don't mom, please."

Somehow, the idea of having my hair cut was more terrifying than anything else that had happened to me in the past few weeks. It was an emotional thing for me, and I'd been clinging to it since my father passed away when I was a child. He'd always liked me with long hair, braiding it in the mornings. Something that most little girls had their mother do.

"Shut up," mom told me roughly, digging in the cabinet until she came back with a pair of scissors. "Don't fight this, Lily. I don't want your blood all over my tiles."

She started cutting the knots from my hair and I sobbed into my hands, feeling the weight of my hair falling down at my feet. The water was somehow even colder now, biting me in a way that it felt like needles were being pushed deep into my skin.

"There we go," she finally announced a while later.

By that time, my body was completely numb from the cold water and she still wasn't done. She scrubbed me clean with a rough loofah, and I found myself staring at her.

"You never cared about me," I said, and she merely rolled her eyes.

"Be quiet," she told me.

"You didn't," I said, louder this time. "All you care about is yourself and making sure your reputation is fucking flawless."

"Don't curse," she smacked me with the loofah. "It doesn't befit you."

"Law likes it," I snapped angrily, giving her a challenging look.

She stared at me, her eyes fiery with anger as she leaned down to me.

"Of course he does," she said viciously. "He always liked barely legal, dirty fucking sluts."

My eyes teared up again and I looked away so she wouldn't notice, but it was too late. She was already grinning like she'd won another fight. I despised this back and forth between us. It had always been the same. Whenever I thought I had the slight upper hand, she would pull the rug out from under me.

Despite the way she was doing it, this might have been the most attention my mother had shown me in at least a decade.

When she was done scrubbing me, she finally shut down the icy water, and I breathed a sigh of relief. Next came the towels, fluffy and soft and so pleasant against my skin I wanted to wrap myself up in one and retreat back into the cellar. It was the only place I felt safe in now.

Mom made me towel off and put lotion on me, reaching every spot of my skin, even the ones that made me flush with embarrassment when she touched them. She was cold about it, like she wasn't even with her own daughter.

Once that was done, she presented me with an outfit to wear, and I gave her a doubtful look.

"You can't be serious."

"Get it the fuck on, Lily," she snarled at me. She'd begun heating a curling iron for my hair and she pointed it at me. "We don't want to add any scars to you tonight, do we? Your Daddy wouldn't like it."

The last part was said with a roll of her eyes.

I couldn't believe her words. This was my own mother.

It felt like I would never stop crying, but I bit my bottom lip to stop myself from screaming out for Law as I put on the clothes she wanted me to wear.

She dried my hair and curled it, putting it into pigtails which I was sure made me look absolutely fucking ridiculous. My hair, which had been down to my butt only half an hour ago, was now shoulder-length in its curls. I bet it made me look younger, something I'd always hated.

When she was done, she took a step back and smiled to herself.

"Perfect," she murmured.

I would've been happy about her compliment, but in truth, I felt like a lamb being taken to the slaughterhouse. I crossed my arms in front of my body as she grabbed me by the elbow and dragged me out of the bathroom toward the living room.

When we were going through the house, I caught a glimpse of myself in the mirror in our hall, and made mom stop to look at it. I didn't even recognize myself.

My face, which had been scrubbed clean, was like a child's. I'd always looked younger without makeup, but now my skin was glowing from the rough scrub, my cheeks blushing and bright and my eyes innocent without the mascara and eyeliner I usually used.

My hair was much shorter, in perfect little girl curls and pinned up into two pigtails with pink silk bows. I was wearing the ridiculous outfit she'd chosen for me—a bright pink pinafore dress over a white blouse, white stockings and a stupid pair of satin pink ballet flats.

"I look like a child," I told my mother disgustedly, and it made her smile as she dragged me through the house.

The fact that she was pleased about that made me really, really scared.

As soon as we came into the living room, I was aware of his presence. Law jumped up from the couch and came toward me. He stopped for a second when he saw what mom had put me in, and a displeased growl tore itself from his lips.

He forced my mother's arm off me and pulled me to stand beside him. I'd never been with him in a setting as normal as that room, and it made my body tingle with excitement. As soon as he joined us, I felt safer.

Safer, and so much fucking needier.

"What the hell have you done to her?" he snarled at my mom. "She looks like a damn doll."

"Perfect," mom chirped, and by the way Law's hand tightened around my arm, I knew he wanted to hurt her. "Just what they'll want."

"You cut her fucking hair?"

"Maybe I wouldn't have had to," mom sneered. "Had you brought her a damn brush."

I smoothed my curls self-consciously, stepping to the side and hoping I didn't look as awkward as I felt.

"Lily," Law said roughly, never taking his eyes off mine. "Wait in the hall."

"Yes, Lily," mom mocked him. "Wouldn't want you to see Daddy lose control."

Law shoved me out of the room and I stumbled into the hallway as the door to the living room banged shut.

I looked at the front door. One I'd unlocked so many times. I could leave right then and there, and neither of them could stop me.

But instead, I sat on a bench in the hall with my heart pounding.

Good girl, Law's words replayed in my mind.

And I realized I'd fallen for him completely.

CHAPTER 16

Law

"THAT'S ENOUGH, EMILY," I SAID the moment the door closed behind Lily.

It was a struggle keeping my voice level when all I wanted to do was snap and roar at her before tearing her smugly simpering head right off her shoulders. I'd never hated someone as much as I did her, and it's not like I've gone through life making close friendships.

"Enough of what, Lawson?" she asked, playing that innocent game she was so good at and that annoyed me so much.

I knew damn well that she was doing it just to piss

me off. What she had to gain from it though, I couldn't be sure yet.

"You know what I'm talking about. Stop fucking around with Lily."

"I think it's you that's fucking around with my daughter," she said shortly, snorting.

"Really? That's the way you want to play it?" I asked. "I thought we had an understanding, Emily."

"So did I. I told you she needs to be ready to be seen in public. We have a very important dinner tomorrow evening and I want her to look her best for it. Since you were doing nothing about it, I took it into my own hands. Never trust a man with a woman's job."

She shrugged her shoulders nonchalantly and I had to take deep breaths to keep from going over to her and showing her exactly what I thought about what she was doing. Not only had she humiliated Lily and scarred her probably more than I had managed so far, she had done so without talking to me first. Lily was mine and Emily was going to lengths to disobey that simple truth.

"I'm not going to let you sell her to anyone," I said, teeming.

I had to get out of this house and I had to get Lily out of this house before something I might regret happened.

"We'll see about that," she responded curtly, giving me

a look that spoke volumes. She was expecting me to fall in line and I was expecting her to do the same.

Neither one of us would budge, that much was clear.

For the umpteenth time, the vision of just killing her and dumping her body somewhere where only wild dogs could find it came to my mind. Yet my hand wouldn't rise to do it. As vile and evil as this woman was, she was my babygirl's mother. Even though Emily certainly wasn't worthy of that title.

I didn't react to that, just shaking my head and walking past her. She stopped me at the door, speaking up.

"Where do you think you're going?"

"I'm taking her out of the house," I said, not sparing her a look.

"No, you're not!" she practically screeched.

I had to admit, it gave me a sick sense of satisfaction to get a rise out of her.

"You were the one saying she needed to be ready to be seen in public. Do you want her shaking like a leaf when someone sees her, when your important friends see her? I don't think so. The best way to make sure that it doesn't happen is to get her used to being seen and talked to again."

"But someone might recognize her," Emily argued.

All I could do was scoff at that.

"You were the one adamant about her being seen. That comes with the inherent risk of being recognized, darling."

I didn't have to look at her to know she prickled at that. Regardless, she huffed and the clatter of her high heels led away as I slipped into the front hall, finding Lily sitting there like a good girl.

I glanced at the front door, realizing that she could have run if she'd wanted to and this time, she chose not to. It got a slight smile out of me, knowing that she'd trusted me so much even with what her mother had done to her behind my back.

"Babygirl, we're going to go out now," I told her, reaching out my hand to her while grabbing my car keys from the hook with the other.

"Go?" she asked, wide-eyed as she looked up from her ridiculous pink ballerinas.

While I hated that her mother had chosen the clothing for her, I liked the way she looked in them. A far cry from the provocative, dangerously misguided young woman I'd kept an eye on over social media. She looked pure, like I knew she was deep down inside.

"Yes, we're going to go outside."

Tentatively, she took my hand and I unlocked the front door, leading her out. Her steps were timid as she followed me and I took her through the yard to my large black Dodge Ram 1500 pickup truck. I opened the passenger door for her and helped her inside, her expression slightly blank.

I chuckled, patting her knee as I pulled the seatbelt over her and snapped it shut. The desire to let my hand roll higher along her soft inner thigh was maddening, but I knew I had to get both of us away from here, even for a little while, to clear her head. Maybe then...

"It's okay, Lily. You're safe. Give Daddy a smile now."

She nodded and gave me a little smile just like I'd asked. I closed the door and moved around the truck, hopping into the driver's seat. I could have bet good money on the fact that Emily was staring out of a window right now, making sure I actually had the audacity to remove her daughter from her household.

I turned the key in the ignition and the powerful truck roared to life. As I pulled out of the driveway, Lily couldn't stop looking at me in amazement.

"We're... actually going to go away?"

"Yes, like I said. We're going to go out. Together."

She nodded flatly, and when we were a few blocks away from the house, I could almost feel the way her body relaxed in the seat. I knew she had to be on edge from everything that had happened over the last few weeks, from having her life turned upside down, but maybe I hadn't realized just how much the place that it was happening at affected her.

Her hands twirled through her shorter hair as we rode through the streets, making our way downtown.

"I'm sorry she did that to your hair," I said lightly, reaching my hand out to touch her hair.

The slightest quiver ran through her lower lip, but she shook her head then.

"It's okay. It'll grow back."

My little fighter, I thought, smiling.

She was tougher than she looked, and that was a good thing. I got the feeling that she was going to need to be strong to get through what was still on the horizon.

I vowed to myself that this was the last time I would let Emily do anything to her. From now on, it was all on me. I couldn't fail Lily again.

First order of business—giving her a happy day.

CHAPTER 17

Lily

B EING OUTSIDE OF THE CELLAR was good for me. For us.

I could tell that Law was troubled, and I did my best to distract him. He seemed to get in a better mood every time I giggled or hugged him close as we waked through town. I knew something was brewing inside his mind, but for now, all that mattered was that we were together.

He led me into store after store and helped me pick out things I would like. When we passed a lingerie store, I didn't have to beg for too long for him to take me inside, even though I could tell how much he loved me whispering 'daddy, please' into his ear.

We dismissed the help of a sales assistant and instead, I asked Law to pick out things for me to wear.

"I want Daddy to choose my outfits for him," I whispered in his ear, and his dark expression was momentarily replaced by a smile. "Please... I want to see what you'd like me to wear."

"Okay, sweetie," Law said. "Let's find some pretty things for my baby to wear."

I giggled and laughed as he led me through the store. I was sure we were attracting some stares, but I didn't give a shit.

There was something about the game we were playing, something about pretending to be a little girl, that made me as wet as it did happy. While it had freaked me out when my mother had dressed me like this, it felt sort of nice being this picture of fragility around Law. It was comforting, being an innocent little girl in a big bad world out to hurt me. And somehow, I knew Law would protect me with his life.

And I trusted mine with him.

Law wouldn't stop until he had an armful of frilly pretty things, and I giggled as he showed me toward the changing rooms. An annoyed assistant stopped us at the door, and my expression fell.

But Law slipped her a hundred-dollar bill without a word, and just like that, he was allowed inside with me. I took his hand and led him into the boudoir-style changing room, making me laugh as I wiggled my butt at him.

I picked the most private changing room and winked at Law before closing the door on him.

"No peeking!" I told him, and he raised an eyebrow at me.

"Babygirl..." he muttered, "I'll look at what's mine whenever the fuck I want to."

I gave him a mean look and he laughed, shaking his head.

"Fine, whatever you say."

"And no cheating, Daddy," I told him pointedly before disappearing behind the door.

I wiggled out of the outfit my mom had chosen for me, incredibly relieved to be out of the clothes she'd picked for me. It wasn't that they were girly or too young—I had liked Law's expression when he saw me in them.

It was the fact my mom had picked them out for me. And as time went on, I realized more and more that she wasn't a good person.

Neither was Law, of course. But somehow, I could forgive him for whatever he'd done to me, and I couldn't do the same for my mom. The look in her eyes when she'd been scrubbing me raw kept replaying in my head, and it was upsetting me. She looked at me with contempt and so much hatred, it was hard to believe she really was my mom.

I picked up the first set Law had picked for me. A pastel blue bra with a lacy thong and a garter belt to go with it. I wouldn't have picked it out myself, but somehow, it was perfect.

I slipped into the set, pinching my cheeks to make them blush even more before posing in front of the mirror. Hands on the wall and my ass toward the door.

"Daddy!" I called out.

The door of the changing room flew open and I giggled at him, wiggling my butt toward Law's figure in the mirror.

"Jesus Christ," he said, closing the door behind him. "Come here, you little slut."

I laughed and tried to get away in the changing room, but his strong arms wrapped around me and pulled me back into his embrace.

"What did I say about running away, sweetheart?" he growled in my ear, and I stopped play-fighting when his fingers wrapped around my throat.

"Daddy," I whispered. "Daddy, please."

"What is it, babygirl?" he asked me. "Scared?"

His fingers tightened when I shook my head no.

"I want Daddy to play with me," I whispered. "I'm gonna ruin these panties if you don't."

He cursed out loud and his free hand roamed to my thigh. I moaned as he caressed the tender skin there.

"You want me to fuck you here?" he asked me roughly.

"Yes," I whimpered softly. "I want Daddy to make me ride his cock and let me play like a big girl."

He let go of me then, and I stumbled forward, giving him a worried look. Maybe I'd gone too far.

"Lily," he said sternly. "What kind of game are you playing?"

I forced myself to look into his eyes.

"I thought you liked me that way," I whispered. "I thought you liked it when I was your little girl."

"Yeah, but..."

He hesitated, his eyes mesmerized and worried at the same time. I stood up straighter, showing off the little ensemble I was wearing and making him curse out loud.

"Fuck, Lily," he said. "I didn't think you liked it, though."

I moved toward him, rubbing against his chest with my tits pushed out.

"Me neither. But it's kind of hot... isn't it?" I said, pulling on the ends of my pigtails and giving him an innocent pouty-faced look. "Doesn't Daddy wanna feel how wet my pussy is?"

He grabbed me by the hips, forcing my head down until I gasped. He kicked my feet apart gently, bending me at the waist so I could see us both in the mirror.

"This is fucking mine," he told me, running his fingers down my back and smacking my ass.

"Shhh!" I laughed, and he grinned at me in the mirror.

"Don't shhh me, little girl," he groaned. "You're gonna get in fucking trouble."

His fingers rolled over my ass, making me gasp. He forced his way between my legs, playing with the little piece of fabric between my ass cheeks and making me cry out.

"That feels good, doesn't it, sweetheart?" Law cooed at me. "You like Daddy playing with your little panties?"

"Yes Daddy!" I pushed my ass out toward him, shaking it for him.

"Time to see if my little girl's wet for me," he muttered, and I took a deep breath as he rapped his knuckles against my pussy and sighed.

"You know, I really like this thong on you," he told

me thoughtfully. "I think I'm gonna buy it. But only if you make a pretty wet spot on it first, babygirl."

"But the sales lady's gonna see!" I giggled, pretending to be horrified.

"Let her," Law smiled at me in the mirror. "Let her wonder what happened."

"But I want Daddy to fuck me," I whined.

"Maybe," he said. "But you don't get to take the thong off until I see a fucking wet spot from your little cunt, babygirl."

I exhaled as he rubbed me through the lace, big, strong fingers teasing my clit through the fabric and making me push my hips back out at him.

"Daddy," I gasped. "Push it aside, please..."

My back arched as of its own accord, my body unable to stay down with his fingers abusing me like that.

"Be a good girl, Lily," he grunted at me. "And stay the fuck down."

His free hand went to the small of my back, holding me down. I braced my hands against the wall and tried to stifle my moans as he played with my pussy.

"Daddy, please." My voice was getting louder and more desperate. "I need something inside me."

"Okay, baby," he said, and I moaned in delight when

his fingers prodded inside the panties, outlining the lips of my pussy and making me mewl. "You need something in here? What if it hurts?"

"Force it in, Daddy," I begged.

"What if you beg me to stop?" he demanded.

"Keep going 'cause you know I want you to," I said.

He grunted and pushed four fingers inside me. I went crazy, bucking my hips at him from the sudden intrusion, my ass grinding against his wrist as he fucked my cunt.

"Yes, Daddy," I cried out. "More, please more."

"Good girl, Lily," he told me, his other hand wrapping around my waist as he stood behind me. "Look at Daddy in the mirror. Watch me as I make you cum, babygirl."

I looked at our reflections, soft little moans escaping my lips as he worked my pussy. I could feel my orgasm building up, desperate and sweet and inescapable. My gaze was glued to his reflection, desperate to see Law's crazed eyes in the mirror.

"Daddy I'm gonna cum," I cried out. "Please, Daddy, it's too much!"

"Come on, sweetheart," he grunted. "Just let it all go for Daddy."

He curled his fingers up inside me and I almost collapsed on his hand. I felt myself gushing, my pussy dripping all over his hand and making me sob because it was so fucking much to take.

"Good girl," he whispered against my hair, stroking my clit while I tried to stifle my cries. "You liked squirting for Daddy, didn't you, babygirl?"

"Y-yes, Daddy," I whispered, slowly realizing that was what had happened.

I felt deeply embarrassed for some reason, and when Law slid his fingers out of me, I avoided his gaze. He forced my chin up when I tried to look away.

"Lily," he said roughly. "You don't look away from me. Ever."

"I'm sorry, Daddy," I muttered, barely able to look him in the eye.

"Are you okay?" he wanted to know, and I blushed in response. "Is my little girl embarrassed Daddy made her squirt in here?"

I looked away and he laughed, grabbing me in his arms and parting my lips with the hand that had been inside me.

"No little girl of mine is gonna be embarrassed about that, Lily," he promised me roughly. "Because that was fucking amazing, and I can't wait to do it again. Now, Lily, why don't you lick my fingers clean so you see how good your sweet pussy tastes?"

I looked into his eyes as I took one finger after the other and licked them clean.

"Good fucking girl," he grunted. "Now get dressed and come outside so Daddy can spoil you."

A minute later, we passed the bright red sales assistant. I kept my eyes trained on the floor, mortified to hell and back, as Law passed her the basket of the underwear I'd tried on.

"We'll take everything," he said simply, and I erupted in a fit of giggles, making him laugh back and squeeze me closer.

Once we'd paid, we walked out of the store with Law's hand wrapped around my waist. He kissed me on the lips, gentle but demanding, and looked at his watch.

"Alright, babygirl," he said with a sigh. "Time to get back home."

I froze on the spot, giving him a hurt look. It was like he was breaking the spell, and I really, really didn't want him to, because it opened up too many questions.

Would I go back to the cellar when we came to the house?

Was he sleeping with his wife at the same time—my mother?

Would he treat me like this from now on, or was I back to being a prisoner?

"I don't want to," I said, the little girl act disappearing into thin air. "I don't want to go back there."

"Why, babygirl?" Law asked me, his voice surprisingly gentle.

I thought about it for a second before saying, "I don't want to be around her."

"Your mom?" he wanted to know, and I nodded.

"I don't like her living there with us," I admitted. "I don't care if you put me in the cellar, I just don't want to be around her anymore."

He pondered my words, then tugged on my pigtails playfully.

"Duly noted," he said. "Now come on, Lily, it's bedtime for little girls like you."

CHAPTER 18

Law

THE NEXT MORNING, I CAME home early from a quick round of checking up on my construction sites around town. I was still on a high from my day with Lily, the memories of making her squirt all over my hand in the lingerie store playing on a loop in my brain. We'd followed it up with another session when we got back to the cellar, but that moment was too special not to focus on.

It signaled complete release and trust from Lily, and that was the greatest prize I could imagine.

I barely noticed the flashy Jaguar that was parked behind the house. It wasn't Emily's, but usually her guests parked in front of the house. I frowned to myself but thought nothing of it, going inside the house. I needed a quick shower and after that, I was planning on going down to Lily to spend my day with her in preparation for the dinner.

We might not be able to get out of it, but I sure as hell was going to make sure we were in the best mood we could be in leading into it.

I moved through the house and was almost at the door to my study when I heard a high-pitched moan coming from one of the bedrooms. A part of me wanted to ignore it—maybe it was just Emily getting off on her own, thinking I wasn't home, and that was not something I wanted to witness—but my curiosity got the better of me. Any leverage I could gain over Emily was worth its weight in gold right now.

As I got closer, instinctively making sure my steps were soundless, I could make out two female voices, moaning and giggling and gasping. A smile spread over my lips as I realized one of them was definitely Emily's.

The Jaguar was starting to make a lot more sense now.

Right in the middle of a pitchy scream, I pulled the

door to the master bedroom—the room Emily had insisted I sleep in with her at the beginning of our marriage—to reveal Emily in bed with Julie.

Emily's ass was in the air, her head buried between Julie's legs, lapping at her cunt, with both women writhing. Julie was the one screaming, her hands clutching Emily's hair. I couldn't hold back my laughter.

Both of them scrambled like cats being sprayed by a hose. Julie grabbed a blanket to cover her tits, mortified, but Emily just sat up and smoothed back her hair. Her face was draining of color. I think this might have been the first time anyone had ever seen Emily embarrassed.

I was glad to be witness to that.

"Don't mind me," I said, casually leaning against the wall with the widest smile possible on my lips. "Keep doing what you were doing, ladies. I enjoy a good show as much as the next man. Are you taping this for Kent?" I asked, cocking a brow at Julie.

Her mouth fell open and she scooched closer to Emily.

"Kent can't know about this," she muttered, her words barely audible, but I caught them well enough.

"Oh, he can't?" I asked, crossing my arms over my chest. "Now ain't that a problem."

"Get the fuck out," Emily hissed at me.

With a theatric sigh, I turned on my heel and did as she asked of me. I had all the information I needed.

I had to wonder if Julie did, though. Knowing Emily, I was certain she didn't have a genuine bone in her body. There was no way that the good time she was showing Julie was for any other reason than to get closer to her wealthy, depraved husband.

But who was I to judge? Maybe sweet little Julie was just as bad as Emily was.

Deciding to forego my shower, I whistled a tune as I headed down the stairs with the plan to go straight to Lily now. Emily caught me as I was about to round the staircase.

"Lawson!" she whispered urgently, wrapped up in another sheet and the door to the bedroom safely shut. "What the fuck are you doing here?"

It was a day of firsts. I wasn't sure if I'd heard Emily curse before. She had to be really pissed off to let her carefully maintained façade fall like that. The good fortunes just kept ramping up, didn't they? "What do you mean, dearest? I'm in my own home! I think I should be the one asking you what you're doing, fucking a woman in our marriage bed."

I could barely keep from laughing straight in her face.

"It's not a marriage bed if we've never fucked," she said shortly. Another thing that bothered her, I guess—I'd never made a move on her, and she'd badly wanted me to. I wasn't dumb enough to give her power over me like that. "You can't tell anyone about what you saw. Promise me."

"I don't owe you any promises," I told her, feeling the bitter edge of aggravation flaring again. She had no right to ask me to do anything for her. "But I think it's about time you reassess your plans with Lily, Emily. Wouldn't want Kent to know what his lovely wife is doing behind his back, now would we? Or are you fucking him as well?"

It wouldn't surprise me in the least.

Her expression changed, the note of panic slowly seeping away and being replaced by cold, hard determination. I knew that look. Fuck, I'd perfected that look.

"Listen here, Lawson. Don't even try to interfere with my plans. I can make you disappear, you and that brat of mine both, and not in the way that you would like. I can destroy both of you, and I can make you watch as I tear Lily into pieces. Fall in line or be made to fall in line. Not a fucking word out of you."

Her blue eyes flashed with icy hatred. She turned around and headed back toward the bedroom, the dramatic statement of her exit slightly marred by the long sheet dragging behind her, and the fact that her chin still glistened with Julie's juices.

I stood there for a moment, feeling dark clouds gathering around me. As much as I would have like to think otherwise, I knew that Emily wasn't the kind of woman to not back her threats up. She wasn't just all words.

My insides twisted, the battle between knowing I had enough on her to make her be more careful, and also realizing that she had enough on me to turn my life and Lily's into pure hell, battling within me. All I knew for certain was that I had to get Lily out of the house. Now. Before Emily could really sit down and fucking think about what had just happened.

Making my mind up on the spot, I rushed to Lily's room, where her mother had stashed the suitcase and the things she'd had with her when she came home. I found a smaller bag in one of the closets and threw some necessities in there, not stopping to really pick and choose, but making sure that she had what she needed.

Then, I put the suitcase back the way it had been, zipping it up, and grabbing the smaller bag with me. The keys to Lily's cell were in my hands long before I reached the door to her room. As soon as I pulled the door open, finding Lily looking at me expectantly and wearing that sweet smile of hers that I'd seen more and more as of late, I knew I was doing the only right thing.

Consequences be damned, I was getting her out of here.

"We're leaving," I told her sharply. "Now."

I grabbed her hand and yanked her along with me before she could say a word or ask a single question. We didn't have time for that. Julie was probably throwing her clothes on as she spoke, trying to get out of the house as fast as she could, and I knew that the moment we were alone, the gears in Emily's head would start turning.

I needed to make sure that we were far away from her by the time that happened.

Without really knowing where we were going, or what we were going to do next, I practically dragged Lily up the stairs and to my truck.

I have to make sure she's safe.

CHAPTER 19

Law

LILY KEPT THROWING QUESTIONING GLANCES at me as we drove, but this time they weren't laced with the kind of jittery nervousness they had been when we went to town. For lack of a better name for it, this time it felt like she was... worried about me.

Not that I could blame her. I came off as little more than erratic, dragging her out of the house without so much as an explanation. It didn't help that for the first hour or so, I wouldn't respond to any of her questions and circled the town, trying to come up with a plan that would end up with both of us being happy.

Or if not happy, then at least moderately content.

The sad truth was, there was no such option.

Finally, I chose a direction and headed out of town, toward the mountains. The sun was starting to set and I felt my phone ring incessantly in my pocket. It had to be Emily. I reached for it and shut off the phone, throwing it in the small compartment under the radio. I wasn't going to be at her beck and call, at least not tonight.

The roads were getting more winding as the altitude started to increase, my big truck managing the change easily enough. My mind was barely on the drive, taking the familiar curves with a practiced ease as I rattled my brain, trying to coax something, anything better out of the recesses of my mind than what I was thinking right then and there.

"Law, please," Lily said after a long silence, having opted for giving me the quiet I'd clearly asked for. "Can you tell me what's going on? Where are we going? Daddy, please..."

It was the last part that broke through to me.

I glanced at her, her hair loose now, hovering just above her shoulders, her big blue eyes shining with worry. There was no fear there though. I wasn't sure if she was putting on a brave face for me, realizing that things were off, or whether she hadn't figured out that something bad was happening.

Who was I kidding? She was doing it for my benefit.

With an exhale, I shook my head.

"It's complicated."

Lily laughed, her cheeks flushing slightly.

"Right, because it never is otherwise. Everything leading up to now has made complete sense!" she jested. "Come on, please tell me. Not that I mind getting out of the house, but... I don't think this was exactly planned?"

She put a hand on my thigh and I covered it with my wide palm, squeezing her hand.

"We're almost there," I said, turning off the narrow road into a thatch of greenery, the forest quickly engulfing us.

A few minutes later, a small cabin came into view, illuminated by the light of the headlights. It wasn't much, but it was mine... and I hoped that Emily didn't know about it.

"Where are we?"

"My place," I told Lily, killing the engine and getting out.

I grabbed Lily's suitcase from the back and helped her out, squeezing her hand again as I led her to the house. The key was under the mat—I didn't want to risk keeping one on my keychain, lest Emily ask about it. I set down the suitcase and unlocked the door, striding into the darkness as soon as I could.

The electricity had to be turned on separately but when the lights flooded the living room, Lily was caught standing right under them, looking around in wonder. A smile spread over her lips immediately.

"It's not much," I said, feeling suddenly self-conscious about where I'd brought her.

Somehow, keeping her in a cellar surrounded by dirt and grime seemed better than bringing her into a house that could have been luxurious, but instead was strictly functional.

"It's perfect," she said, running her fingers over the quilt on the couch and going to look out of one of the windows.

I closed the door and locked it behind her, propping the small suitcase up against one of the chairs.

"It used to be a hunting lodge for a local rich prick. He died and his wife sold it off. I bought it for cash... I haven't changed it much," I explained, not sure why I was trying to fill the silence.

Lily looked at me and grinned, looking like a woman in control of her destiny. Maybe it was the way she was handling this, or maybe it was just because I still wasn't used to seeing her out of situations carefully controlled and maintained by me, but she was mesmerizing.

"I don't mind," she said, coming up to me and snaking her hands around me. "How long can we stay?"

"You can stay until tomorrow morning," I said softly, kissing her on the forehead.

I untangled myself from her gingerly and put distance between us, heading for the small kitchen.

"Do you want some tea?" I asked.

Lily, looking surprised at my sudden exit, followed me a few paces behind.

"Sure, I guess."

She leaned against the doorframe, watching me fuss around with the kettle and the cups. I knew I was just trying to prolong the inevitable. I knew what I had to do... I just didn't want to do it.

"Are you going to tell me what's going on?" she asked again as I handed her a mug of steaming tea and led her back to the couch.

Together, we took our seats and I rolled the cup between my palms, looking down at the dark brown liquid. My heart was resisting what my brain was telling me was the right thing... for once, I would have to listen to my head over my mind.

"I walked in on your mother today with someone else."

Lily's expression barely budged, but her attention was squarely on me. I could tell that she was trying to read my face for any sign of what I felt about it.

"Were you... jealous?" she asked, her tone carefully neutral.

I snapped my gaze up to her face quickly and set down the mug on the coffee table. Putting my hands around her, I gently pulled her to me.

"Of course fucking not. She means nothing to me, never has. What I meant was that I caught her in bed with someone she shouldn't have been with. A woman, the wife of a buyer that she's been trying to get close to... We had an altercation and I felt I had to get you out of the house."

Lily relaxed against me, nodding faintly.

"Okay," she said. "I don't mind. I'm happy to be with you wherever we go."

Without even knowing it, she was making this so much harder.

A large part of me wished that she hated me, that she despised me right now and would do anything in her power to get away from me. But she'd already shown with staying in the entryway yesterday that she was done with running, at least from me.

And now I was going to have to tell her to do it, just when she'd decided she wouldn't.

"We can't stay here together," I told her, and it took every ounce of my stubborn determination to grind those words out.

It felt like I was shooting myself in the fucking face, just by uttering those words.

"What?!" Lily asked, straightening up immediately and training her gaze on mine. "What do you mean? If we can't stay at my mother's house then we'll be here... or somewhere else! Anywhere else! It doesn't matter as long as we're together."

I wished I could agree with her.

"It's not that simple. Your mother has more than enough to call a manhunt on me. I have a track history... Law enforcement might not know me under this name, but you don't go through life doing the shit I've done without getting a couple files on you. If you get caught with me, that just means they'll turn you back over to her and I can't let that happen."

The image of Chloe seemed to superimpose itself over Lily for a moment and I felt like I was looking at both of them. I had failed Chloe by letting her go... but as much as I didn't want to admit it, I knew I would be failing Lily if I didn't let her go. It was the hardest choice I'd ever had to make.

"They won't catch us," Lily said, her face ashen as she squeezed my hand. "I know we can make it. I have some money saved up and-"

"No, babygirl, I won't risk your life just because I don't want to let you go. It's going to have to be like this. I'll go back to the house tonight and deal with Emily. You sleep here and then tomorrow morning, at 6:30, there's a bus that stops right next to the exit that led to the house. You can take that and it'll take you out of state.

"I packed a bag for you and I can give you some cash. You'll have to promise me that you'll run as far as you can and you'll never look back. You'll be a good girl and do that for Daddy, right?"

CHAPTER 20

Lily

"YOU'LL BE A GOOD GIRL and do that for Daddy, right?"

The words echoed in my mind and I bit my bottom lip to stop myself from crying out. He couldn't be serious. After everything that had happened, he was just going to ditch me?

I started shaking as I realized he was serious. He really was going to let me go, leave me just like that.

"You're just going to leave me?" I asked. "Don't you... want to be with me?"

"It doesn't matter, Lily," Law told me roughly. "None

of it matters. I just want to keep you out of harm's way, keep you safe."

Keep you away from your mother.

We both knew that was what he meant, even though neither of us said it out loud.

He couldn't do this to me.

Law came closer, his finger pulling on my lip gently.

"It's for the best, little one," he told me calmly. "You're safer without me. You'll do well on your own. You're confident, beautiful, smart. They're going to eat out of the palm of your hand, trust me, babygirl."

He paused for a moment, thinking about his next words.

"Maybe you'll even meet someone your age."

I felt anger now, white hot anger searing my body and making me back away into the corner while I gave him the most evil look I could find in my repertoire.

"I thought you cared about me," I said in an accusatory tone. "I thought you weren't going to let anything bad happen to me."

"I'm not," Law reminded me. "I'm trying to keep you safe. I'm not doing this because I'm selfish, Lily."

I knew he wasn't lying, but I couldn't stop spewing abuse at him. I was upset, my heart beating out of order and tears gathering in the corners of my eyes. I didn't understand it. He was someone I was supposed to hate, and instead, I was breaking at the notion of not spending eternity in his fucked-up care. Probably chained up somewhere in a dim, grimy basement.

"Yeah, sure." I spat the words out at him. "You don't give a shit about me. You never cared about me in the first place. You just wanted to fucking use me!"

I tried to put distance between us, ripping myself away and trying to walk off. But Law's strong, long fingers wrapped around my forearm before I could move an inch. He gave me a warning look, his eyes darkening.

"Careful, Lily," he reminded me. "Watch that little mouth of yours."

"Let me go," I screeched. "Let go of me, Law!"

He pulled me closer, his breath hot against my face. I wanted his lips on mine, my tongue in his mouth. I wanted to kiss him hard, melt against his touch and let him claim my body.

But instead, I fought him with all my might.

"I think you mean something else," Law breathed against my skin, making me mewl helplessly. "I think you mean, 'thank you, Daddy'."

"No," I hissed at him. "I fucking don't. You're not my Daddy, anyway."

I thought he was going to slap me. All the color drained

from his handsome, chiseled face, and he stared me down roughly.

"Take it back," he growled at me.

I didn't respond.

"Now!"

His words were sharp, rough.

"N-no," I muttered, and it sounded like a question.

Law let go of me like he'd been scalded. I stumbled a few steps back and gave him a wounded look, both scared and excited about what he was going to do next. I knew it was coming, but still, when he told me what to do, my skin erupted in goosebumps.

"Strip. Right the fuck now. Naked."

My hands shook, but despite mouthing off at him earlier, I reached for the buttons on my dress. I kept my gaze stubbornly fixed on his, and Law stared back at me as I slid out of the garment. I was burning up, my cheeks blushing with embarrassment. He was treating me like a cheap whore, but a part of me wanted it. Craved it.

I took off my blouse next, leaving only the set of baby pink underwear. I felt him watching me, hungry wolfish eyes drinking me in and trying to see through the remaining skimpy fabric.

"Every. Thing," he reminded me. "Did I fucking stutter, Lily? Right the hell now."

I took off my bra, but crossed my arms in front of my body protectively. Law paled and in a flash, he was next to me. He pulled something out of his pocket and I saw a glint of metal. A pocket knife.

"You little brat," he snarled at me.

He grasped me by the hips, his thumb hooking into my panties. I was embarrassed by how turned on I'd gotten, how soaking wet my pussy was for him. I was hoping he wouldn't notice, all my attention on the knife in his fingers.

I wasn't scared. I was excited. And that almost scared me more.

He sliced through my panties, the knife gliding through the fabric. He put it back in his pocket and ripped the measly piece of fabric away from my body, exposing me to his greedy eyes.

And then he let go.

I watched in shock as he retreated and sat down on an overstuffed armchair. He looked at me and patted his leg, smiling wide.

"Come here, Lily."

My legs moved of their own accord and before I could stop myself, I was walking toward him. But he shook his finger at me before I could take another step.

"No," he said sternly. "On your knees. Good girls crawl for Daddy."

I pursed my lips and felt contempt for him burn in the pit of my stomach and disappear into thin air as I dropped to my knees. I crawled for him, wiggling my ass as I made my way to him, my head blessedly blank.

In that moment, it didn't matter that I might not see him again, that he might leave me. The only thing that was important was that he was here with me right now.

Once I reached the armchair, I sat on my knees and gave him a fully submissive look.

"Good girl," Law muttered, his hand caressing my hair thoughtfully. "But you misbehaved. You're going to be sorry about that, babygirl."

He tipped my chin back and grinned at my trembling bottom lip.

"Take my belt off," he ordered me. "With your mouth."

I stared at him but knew he wouldn't waver. Finally, I leaned closer and he helped me undo the buckle, pull off the belt. He placed it in my mouth and I stared at him, naked, on my knees with my hands on Law's thighs.

"Offer it to me," he told me. "Ask Daddy to hurt you for being a bad girl."

He reached for the belt in my mouth and I let go in his hand. I felt that familiar spark inside of me, naughty and so very bad but so delicious at the same time. I wanted this, badly.

He uncoiled the belt and in a single motion, pulled me up on his lap.

"Unzip me," he said easily. "Suck Daddy's cock."

I followed the next order with shaky hands, taking out his rock hard dick that was throbbing for me already. My mouth watered when I saw the bead of precum decorating his tip, and I took him between my lips eagerly.

"Good girl," Law cooed, and I could feel his naked hand smoothing over my ass. "Open wide for Daddy, that's a good girl."

I sucked him better this time, deeper and wetter and needier. My complaints turned into soft mewls and little gasps and I was glad we'd managed to put the fight behind us.

Until he slapped my ass.

I yelped, the raw handprint echoing through my body as I glared at Law. He grinned at me and motioned for me to go on, and I hated him as much as I wanted him to keep doing that to me.

"What's my name?" he asked me roughly, pushing his hips up and filling my mouth up with cock. "Tell me, babygirl."

"L-Law," I stuttered with my mouth full, and another slap landed on my ass. Cold, buttery leather this time. His belt.

"What's my fucking name, Lily?" His voice was angry, but I could tell he was holding himself back, my hot little mouth working wonders on his swollen cock. "Answer me, baby."

I filled my mouth with him, right to the brim. I retched from the fullness, from having him touch the back of my throat with the tip of his cock.

"Daddy," I begged instinctively, wanting him to stop.

"Daddy?" he repeated, his cock throbbing between my lips and making me moan out loud. "Is that it, sweetheart? Is that my name?"

"Y-yes," I whimpered, and he stuffed my mouth again, pulling out a second later. Long strings of saliva hung from my mouth as I gasped for air, looking at his beautiful cock.

"Say it," he taunted me. "Tell me what I am, and what you are to me."

I looked at him, disheveled and messy and so wet I was dripping on the armchair.

"You're my Daddy," I said softly. "And I'm Daddy's little slut."

Law groaned, landing another lash of the belt against my ass.

"Ow! What was that for?" I wanted to know.

"Because you don't fucking trust me, Lily," he said

darkly. "I know what's best for you. Now finish your fucking dinner."

I sucked him eagerly as he beat my ass, lashings of the belt making me squirm, and the spanking from his hand almost like a caress afterward. He didn't stop until I knew he was about to cum.

His hand reached for me, one wrapping around my throat, the other pinching my nose. I panicked, flailing as he cooed at me.

"That's okay, babygirl," he said softly. "You've been a very good girl. Daddy just wants to make sure you swallow every drop."

I stopped fighting, my eyes going to his. It was enough to make him groan, and when I ran my tongue along his length, he came with a curse, spilling his hot seed inside my mouth. I drank from his cock greedily, milking him dry with my lips.

He didn't let go of me until I was gasping desperately, only making me swallow all of his hot, salty cum.

And then Law's fingers wrapped around my hair and he pulled me up, settling me into his lap. I ground my pussy on his naked cock while he held me, and tried to take deep, even breaths. His hand was smoothing down my back, and he was whispering sweet little things in my ear.

I wanted him.

I wanted this.

I couldn't stand him leaving.

"Don't go," I begged him softy as he tugged on my hair, toying with the curls that were still intact. "Don't let me go, please."

"I have to." He kissed me, gently and with his eyes closed.

I closed mine too, just so he wouldn't see the tears brimming in them.

Truth be told, Law was the only man to give a shit about me since my father passed away.

Law was a jackass, a kidnapper, a fucking crazy man— of course. But he was also caring, and sweet, and wanted the best for me, whatever it cost. I didn't understand how I could feel that way about him, but with the butterflies in my stomach, it was getting harder and harder to deny my feelings for Law.

And all this now, when he was letting me go.

I leaned against his shoulder and he held me tight. I wrapped my legs around his waist because I needed to feel him as close as possible.

"You're a bad man," I told him softly, and he kissed my forehead.

"I know, babygirl," he said. "You should run as far

away from me as possible. Because I might change my mind someday, and then there won't be a safe place for you in the world."

I pressed myself closer, and finally, I began to understand why I needed to leave.

My mother was the biggest villain here. My fists tightened in hatred as I remembered the way she'd washed me. The way she'd given me up to a complete fucking stranger—and was going to do it again, if Law hadn't stopped her.

"Will she let me be?" I asked Law, and we both knew who I was talking about.

"I made her swear," he muttered. "If she doesn't, I'm going to fucking kill her."

Somehow, I knew he was telling the truth.

"Everything you need is in the suitcase. You can spend the night here, but then you need to get the hell out of here, babygirl."

I couldn't look at him, couldn't even bring myself to admit how upsetting this was to me.

I'd fallen for the monster that lived in the cellar with me. I fell for the man from the shadows.

He held me for a long time. It must've been an hour later that he picked me up as if I weighed nothing, setting me on my feet as I rubbed my tired eyes.

"I have to go, babygirl," he told me, and I looked away.

It was too fucking hard to deal with, too painful to lose the man I was supposed to hate all along. But instead, I'd ended up falling for him like a stupid lovesick puppy that didn't know any better.

"Okay," I said in my smallest voice.

"Okay," Law repeated.

I knew he wouldn't be much for goodbyes, but I could tell he was lingering, trying to prolong these last few moments with me. I decided not to make a scene, trying to be a good girl for him like he'd wanted me to be.

He put the suitcase on the table, unzipping it, and I looked at the items inside. A toothbrush, some clothes, an old teddy bear I used to sleep with every night. He'd packed with care even though he was in a hurry. My heart swelled with emotion.

"I wanted you to have a few things you liked."

I looked away.

He pulled me into a tight hug, his hands moving up and down my back in reassuring motions as I cuddled against him. He murmured this and that into my ear, and I stayed strong for him.

I wanted to stay like that forever. I would've done anything to be able to stay with him, to put this all behind us.

Law pulled away, his eyes boring into mine and making me return the look.

"Stay safe out there, babygirl," he said gently. "It's a big world for a little girl."

"I will," I promised. "For Daddy."

He nodded, and hesitated for a moment. I thought maybe he would change his mind, tell me something that was going to change everything. But in the end, he merely kissed me.

I knew my mouth still tasted like him, but he didn't seem to care. He kissed me like his life depended on it, needy and fast and urgent.

When he pulled away, he didn't look at me again.

We didn't say goodbye. I watched him drive away and my heart broke all over again.

CHAPTER 21

Law

I T WAS A LONG DRIVE back. When I climbed out of the truck, the grand house I was looking at had never felt less like home.

I'd never really considered myself the kind of man that needed, or even wanted a home. But it became more than clear to me now that I would have loved nothing more than to have made a home for myself with Lily. Wherever, however.

That was simply a choice I could no longer make.

Clearing my mind, I took a deep breath of the night air and fished a pack of cigarettes out of the glove compartment before locking the truck. I hadn't needed a smoke since I got my hands on Lily, but I definitely fucking needed one now.

Lighting up, I leaned against the side of the truck and took a deep breath. There were a couple of lights on in the house and I could see Emily's shadow moving past one of the windows. I could bet she was waiting on me to come inside, so she could blow up at me for ruining her dinner.

The fact that Lily was missing was probably a far second problem in her mind.

Shaking my head, I looked at the night sky, the stars clearly visible tonight. As corny as it was, I hoped that Lily was looking at them too at that moment. There wasn't much left connecting us, so grasping for the last tendrils was all the more painful.

The smoke went fast, helping to clog up my brain in another kind of way. I was going to be drinking that night, drinking a lot. I shoved the cigarettes in my pocket and stalked inside, reminding myself that murdering Emily would not be a great idea.

It took more self-control than I would have liked to instill that idea in my head in earnest.

As soon as the front door fell shut behind me, I could hear the clicking of Emily's heels heading toward me. There was no point in trying to race her, it wasn't that big of a fucking house, so I just stopped in the large open space that led to the kitchen and dining room, tracking in mud with my boots. Might as well get this particular shitshow over with fast.

"Lawson!" Emily's voice rang out before she came into view, frantic and high-pitched. "Where the hell were you!?"

She skidded to a halt in front of me, looking impeccably put together as usual, but just a little ragged at the edges. Like she needed a smoke. Or someone to teach her not to be a rabid bitch.

"Are we cursing now? It's not very ladylike, Emily. I don't think I owe you any explanations, *Emily*," I said, my voice sounding far more tired than I wanted it to.

"Oh yes, you fucking do," she said, flushing red in the cheeks. "Where's Lily? We were supposed to have dinner tonight with... well, we were supposed to have dinner and I had to call it off last minute. Do you know how humiliating that is? Where is she, where is my daughter?"

"She's safe," I said, ignoring most of what she was rattling on about. "And you'll have nothing to do with her anymore. She's a grown-up, an adult who can make her own decisions."

Emily's eyes went wide and had I been in a better

mood, it might have even been comical. Shock didn't befit her.

"What did you do, Lawson? Where is she!?"

Emily rushed past me, checking the entryway. She ran out of the house and I could only assume she was going for my truck, expecting to find Lily there. I chuckled, despite the lack of humor in the situation. Getting under her skin was a small, but valuable joy in life.

"I already told you. She's safe. She's far away from you and that's how I intend on keeping it."

"You fucking idiot," she hissed, losing what little cool she had left. "Do you realize what you've done!?"

"I've let her go," I said, feeling my heart constrict in my chest.

Looking at Emily, though, I knew I had done the right thing. The only thing I could have done, keeping in mind what was good for Lily. It was just bitter that what was good for her couldn't be good for me.

"I want a divorce," I muttered, turning away from her and heading toward my office. "I don't think we have anything that needs to be settled anymore."

Emily quieted for a moment, but it didn't last long. I hadn't really expected it to, anyway.

"You're not getting a divorce," she fumed. "Fine, you've

done something to my daughter—I'll find out what, I'll find out where you're keeping her—but there is no way in hell that I'm going to let you ruin what I've built up along with it. She's a loss, but I can manage it.

"If you don't want me to turn your precious babygirl's life into pure hell when I find her then you're going to fall in line. Do you hear me?"

She was screaming at me as I walked away from her, the last words muffled by the closing door. I locked it behind me, and her nails scrabbled against the door handle mere seconds later.

"This isn't over, Lawson!" she yelled.

I couldn't care less.

Dropping into my leather chair, I kicked my filthy boots up on the table and lit another cigarette. The smoke plumed around me as I looked at each and every one of the pictures I had of Lily on my wall, studying the features of her face and her body as if trying to memorize them all over again.

It was a joke. I knew her, I knew every bit of her. When I closed my eyes, I could see her face as clear as day. I didn't need these pictures, and yet they almost felt like the only thing I had left of her.

Reaching for the whiskey bottle on my table, I poured myself a full glass and took a long sip between puffs of the cigarette. The drink burned as it went down my throat, but it didn't burn enough.

Emily didn't linger at the door, picking her battles. She knew she had me by the short hairs when I came back to the house, she might just not have realized it yet. I wasn't really expecting her to say yes to the divorce, but I needed to keep her mad and distracted to buy Lily more time.

So far, it was working. But underestimating Emily would have been a mistake, one that I wasn't planning on making.

The first glass of whiskey disappeared as if into thin air and the second and third didn't fare a lighter fate. Chain smoking and drinking, I kept looking at those pictures, mesmerized.

I could imagine so easily the kind of woman Lily would really grow up to be. She had so much strength in her that I think she never realized she had, her energy spent on acting out and being a brat instead. I was sure that was over now, and it was so fucking bitter that I couldn't witness her blossoming.

But this was for her own good. Having a man like me around her for too long... well, it couldn't lead to anything good, right?

Halfway through the fourth glass, I got up. Holding the tumbler and with a lit cigarette between my lips, I walked over to the wall and one by one, removed each picture from it. I threw them in the trash can until there wasn't a single picture on the wall.

Then, I took the still-lit end of my cigarette and threw it in the trash on top of the pictures. They lit up quickly, the edges starting to scorch and pucker until a flame erupted, engulfing the stack. I watched it quietly, tipping a small toast to it when all that remained were ashes.

I needed to let go, and it was the hardest fucking thing I'd ever had to do. Keeping myself on that track was like pulling teeth, especially when all my body wanted to do was get the fuck out of this house and go back to my babygirl.

For better or for worse, that woman had changed me. I could only hope that what I had done to her hadn't ruined her for life.

CHAPTER 22

Lily

*T*HE HOUSE FELT EMPTY WITHOUT him.

Even though we'd barely spent any time there together, I saw signs of Law everywhere I looked and it made my chest swell with an ache I didn't recognize. It took me a while to figure out what it meant.

I was homesick.

Homesick for the fucking cellar. For the grimy bathroom, for the dirty mattress.

Homesick for Daddy.

I padded around the room with my feet bare, pulling on a fluffy robe I found in the downstairs bathroom. It must have been Law's. I could smell his musky, woodsy scent all over it, and it made me belt it firmly to feel like he was close.

I was aimless and restless, trying to find something to do, something to pass the time. I knew I would have to leave in the morning. My opened suitcase on the table reminded me of that every time I passed it, the contents laid out neatly and folded to perfection, even if the initial packing had been abrupt.

It showed me Law really was trying to take care of me and make sure I was alright. He wanted me to be safe, and we both knew the only way to do that was to get me away from him and my mother.

I made myself something to eat from the stuff I found in the kitchen, just a simple sandwich to tide over my hunger. It felt weird to make my own food, and I realized with a start I missed Law taking care of me, however fucked up it was.

The vastness of the hunting lodge felt constricting for some reason. I didn't know what to do with myself, and I ended up curling up on the sofa with a mug of random tea I'd found in the cupboards.

I inhaled the soothing scent of the chamomile tea brewing, and let it carry me to another time. When I was a little girl and my dad was still around, and he used to make me chamomile tea to calm down my tummy when I wasn't feeling well.

I let my thoughts transport me, and I took small sips of the hot drink as I slowly drifted off to sleep. My head lolled to the side and I set the cup aside, burrowing myself in the blankets on the sofa, leaving all the lights on as I closed my eyes.

Monsters don't bite in the light, right?

* * *

"DADDY, I DON'T FEEL WELL," I GROANED.

He came closer, tucked me under the pink blanket that matched everything else in my room. It was a girly explosion with all kinds of toys, from dolls to tea sets, pink walls, pink fabrics, pink everything. It was the perfect room for a girl my age, and I knew I was the envy of all of my friends.

But right then, I had an awful tummy ache and I wanted my daddy to make me feel better.

"I know, sweetheart," he said, smoothing down my hair. "I don't feel well either. I think I must've caught the bug you got."

He tickled me under the bedspread and I giggled. Then, he passed me a cup of still steaming tea and I took a long sip of the hot liquid.

"That'll make you feel better anytime now," he promised me.

"You should have some too, daddy," I told him sternly, making him laugh out loud. "What? I don't want you to get sick."

"I'll be fine, sweetie," he promised me. "I haven't been feeling well for a little while now. Maybe it's just the stress at work."

"You should see a doctor," I nodded wisely. "Maybe they can give you some medicine and then you'll be all better, like me."

I smiled brightly and my father ruffled up my hair, making me laugh again.

"I promise," he said solemnly, giving me his pinky.

I looped my own finger around his and he gave me a conspiratorial smile.

"I'll go see a doctor next week," he promised, and I nodded, pleased with what he'd said.

"Good, daddy." I gave him a hopeful look. "Can I have a bedtime story?"

"Of course, sweetheart," he said with a smile. "You know I always have time for that, for my favorite girl."

I beamed with pride, somehow feeling victorious over mommy, knowing he'd chosen me over her. Maybe he hadn't said it out loud, but I'd always known daddy thought I was special. He loved me more than mommy, I was sure of it. It shouldn't make me feel as good as it did.

We had to interrupt story time because daddy wasn't feeling well. I could see him squirming in his seat, all the color draining from his face. It was then that mommy knocked on the door of my bedroom, a cup in her hands.

"Hello," she said, her eyes leaving me as she walked toward daddy. "I know you're not feeling well. Thought you might want some tea."

Daddy look strained when she approached us. I knew they'd been fighting a lot—I'd heard them shouting. Mommy even broke some plates one day.

He took the cup from her hands gratefully though, and took a long sip of the tea. Then, he grimaced.

"It's awfully sweet," he said apologetically.

"It'll make you feel better," mommy promised him. "Just drink up."

I thought daddy didn't want to upset her, and he gave me a wink before drinking up the tea. Mommy smiled, looking pleased as she took the cup from him.

"Oh, Arnold," she added over her shoulder almost as an afterthought. "I'm going to need your help in the cellar later."

Our cellar had been unusable since we'd moved in. I hadn't even been down there—mommy said it wasn't safe for little girls. But I knew she wanted to renovate it, and daddy sighed and promised he would help her later.

Mommy left and I gave him a bright smile, hoping he would feel better.

"I'll see you in the morning, princess," he told me, and I nodded as he kissed my forehead. "I promise we'll both be feeling better. Night."

"Night, daddy."

He pulled the sheets up around me and I snuggled into my bed. I was asleep in seconds, but I didn't sleep well.

I woke up an hour later, judging by the clock on my wall I'd just learned to tell time from. My mouth was dry and I needed a glass of water, bad. Someone had turned off all the lights in my room, even the little nightlight, and I stumbled in the darkness, my heart beating too fast. I didn't like the dark.

I padded my way downstairs, into the kitchen. I stopped in the hallway when I heard raised voices. I peeked through the keyhole, looking at what was going on inside.

I could hear mommy and daddy again. They were fighting, I think.

"She's not going to know," mommy said. "She doesn't have to do anything with it."

"It doesn't matter," daddy bit out. "I don't agree. You're not doing it in my fucking house, Emily."

Daddy never cursed, and I covered my mouth in surprise when the word left his lips.

"Whatever," mommy said roughly. "Just check the pipes in the cellar."

"I can't tonight," daddy groaned. "I feel like shit, Em."

"You promised."

Mommy's voice was ominous, and daddy sighed.

I could see him moving through the keyhole, just a hint of his shoulders as he moved to the sealed-off door at the end of the corridor. No one had ever used it, and as far as I knew, it didn't lead anywhere.

Daddy looked at mommy over his shoulder.

"I know you're up to something, Emily," he told mommy.

She scoffed, replying, "Don't be ridiculous."

I stared at daddy watching her thoughtfully, knowing he couldn't see me. And then he opened the door and walked into the darkness.

I never saw him come out.

* * *

I woke up with a start, jumping up from the sofa with my heart beating like crazy. I shook my head and it took me a moment to realize where I was. Once I realized I was safe, with all the lights still on and no one in the house, I pulled my knees up to my chest and furrowed my brows.

That dream... was it really just a dream?

I settled back into the sofa and tried to understand what it all meant. I remembered the first part of the dream—it was the last time I'd seen my dad. The next day when my mother picked me up from school, she explained to me that he was gone. He died in a car accident, it was sudden but he felt no pain. Bottom line was—he was gone.

I'd cried for weeks. I'd never felt close to my mom, and losing my dad felt like even more of a tragedy. There was a small funeral.

I never asked mom which car he'd gotten into an accident with. We had two, and both of them were intact.

I sat on the sofa, trying to put the pieces together. I remembered that night, the tea my father had made me to make my upset tummy feel better. And then mom bringing him something to drink, too.

Could the part from the kitchen be true? I knew now the cellar was being used, something my mother had lied to me about for years. I knew now it was equipped to have a prisoner in there for long periods of time.

But maybe that wasn't the case with my father.

The farther I thought the more I remembered. He hadn't been feeling well for a while before he died. Mom used to give him all kinds of homemade medications to make it better. It never did.

I gasped when I finally came to a conclusion.

Maybe mom wasn't trying to help my father.

Maybe she was trying to poison him.

I jumped up from the sofa, pacing the length of the room as I tried to come to terms with my repressed memories. I'd had nightmares, awful nightmares as a child. They all had to do with monsters in the dark, coming up from the ground, burrowing through the floors of our house and killing me and my whole family.

Maybe the monster lived in the house all along.

I couldn't let the realization affect me too much. I knew now my mother could have been the one who killed my dad. But I also knew that if she caused the death of her child's father, she would stop at nothing to get what she wanted.

And she wanted me, to sell me off and make a fortune now that she had finally found a buyer worthy of her time.

Law was nothing more than a liability.

My face drained of color as I remembered the few times he'd mentioned he wasn't feeling well. That he was feeling sick, that his stomach was upset. How he'd grown paler over his visits in the cellar.

I knew she was trying to do the same thing she'd

done to my father. And I wasn't going to let her get away with it.

I stripped off the robe, letting it fall to the floor as I rummaged in the suitcase for some clothes. I got dressed in a hurry, leaving my hair in those ridiculous ringlets. I realized I had no way of getting out of there—I didn't even know where I was.

But I would walk if I had to, walk and save Law. I needed to make sure he was alright, and I needed to show the world who my mother really was. I was determined as I set off, walking outside to find the world sleepy. It wasn't too late, only around 9:00 p.m.

I still had a chance.

If Law still wanted to send me away after I'd exposed my mother, so be it. At least I would know I'd done everything in my power to convince him of keeping me. At least I'd know I'd saved him from whatever my mother was trying to do to him—and I knew none of it was good news.

Law was the only good thing left in my life, and I needed to make sure he made it through the hurricane of fury that was my mother. Finally, I understood what kind of person she was. What she was capable of to get what she wanted.

I needed to save Law.

I needed to save my Daddy.

CHAPTER 23

Law

"*L*AWSON, PUT THAT OUT," EMILY hissed at me, catching me sneaking a smoke in the kitchen. "You'll stink up the dinner."

"The dinner you so lovingly cooked for us?" I asked her, cocking a brow.

All I got in return was a withering glare as Emily pulled out the roast from the over. She'd just heated it up, everything she was serving that night was from a gourmet chef, delivered earlier in the day with strict instructions on how to finish the courses for serving.

I took two more drags, killing off the cigarette, and

then dropped the butt in a coffee cup that doubled as an ashtray. Emily's nose was wrinkled as she did her best not to look at me, obviously miffed by my 'uncouth' behavior.

I would have been lying if I said it didn't give me some joy to see her pissed off.

"You look like a bum. Red eyes, stinking of cigarette smoke... This is not what we agreed on," she said, pursing her lips.

"Yeah, well, we didn't agree on a lot of shit but here we are, princess," I huffed, grabbing my whiskey glass and heading for the dining room.

It was the day after I'd left Lily in my cabin. Emily had rescheduled the dinner for tonight and I had to be an unwilling accomplice to this society shindig, masquerading as an intimate dinner between two couples. Kent and Julie had arrived more than an hour ago and the level of awkward small-talk was incomprehensible.

Julie could barely look me in the eye, practically twitching whenever I came too close to her and blushing bright red with embarrassment. Emily didn't let it bother her at all, playing the part of the perfect hostess, but obviously investing most of her time in Kent. Rather than his lovely wife, who Emily had been fucking the day before, it seemed that the husband was the prize she was really after.

Which, again, surprised me exactly none at all.

Which only left Kent himself, who as far as I was concerned was the scum of the earth, and I'd known a lot of the scum of the earth, being one myself. It took a lot of work to be valued that low in my mind, but Kent managed to fit the bill.

I'd done my research on the guy, asking around a bit more. I'd known him to be a big buyer of sex slaves before, but now I knew his type. Preferably underage virgins from privileged, white families. Seeing as he kept buying a new girl every six months or so, I doubted any of his 'pets' lasted long enough to ever be heard of again.

This was the kind of man Emily had wanted to sell Lily to. My insides twisted with disgust and rage, the desire to wipe Kent's simpering smile off his face with my fist coming to me the moment I stepped into the room.

"Dinner about done?" Kent asked me conversationally.

I grumbled something akin to a reply back at him, taking a seat at the head of the table.

Julie had been admiring some of the fancy artwork Emily liked buying and then getting rid of when it no longer fit the 'décor' of the room. The moment she saw me being back in the room, she flushed beet red, which with her complexion was a sight to behold.

"Dinner's served!" Emily called out in a sing-songy

voice, carrying in the big roast and setting it down in the middle of the table.

There were scores of food, far more than what four people could realistically eat, even more so considering that both of the women looked like they tried to avoid eating as a general rule of thumb.

"It looks marvelous, Emily," Kent said with a broad grin, looking over the food with an appreciative expression. "Julie, my dear, you should cook for me. A home-cooked dinner warms a man's heart."

Julie mumbled an apology under her breath and Emily stood up straighter and prouder, like a preening peacock. The blatantly obvious pandering to one another that Emily and Kent were doing was sickening. The fact that I had to be a part of it only added insult to injury.

"You flatter me," Emily said lightly, doing nothing to divert the attention from her.

Obviously satisfied, she took her seat and piled small quantities of the food that 'she' had prepared on her plate, passing the bowls around. I wasn't hungry, but I obliged the general theme of this charade and grabbed some food as well, filling my plate.

What I really wanted was another smoke, which probably anyone could guess just by being in the same room with me. I reeked of nicotine and alcohol, even after a long, hot shower, but I couldn't care less. It was Emily who kept giving me disapproving glances, though, and that made it all worth it.

If I embarrassed her in front of her lover and the vile piece of shit of a man whose wallet she was trying to crawl into, it would make my day.

"I'm not saying anything that shouldn't be said," Kent said smugly.

That prick was just begging to get his teeth kicked out.

I tried to tune out the conversation as much as I could, and it seemed I wasn't the only one. I could barely taste the food in my mouth and my head was a muddled mess, but I still seemed to be having a better time than Julie. Though she was dressed in a black gown fit for a gala, she almost disappeared into the backdrop, not uttering a word.

My attention shifted to her as Kent and Emily kept dancing around one another with dumbass compliments and little anecdotes and stories, filling the air with endless small-talk. Julie, however, barely touched her food and most of the time she was staring at the table right in front of her, scraping the nails of her left hand over her thighs when she thought no one would notice.

The dinner was the epitome of awkward, but even in my sullen state, I realized that there was something off with Julie. I didn't know whether it was just the fact that

I'd walked in on her and Emily, or that she had to share a dinner table with her husband, Emily and me, but she looked completely off-kilter.

And neither her husband nor her lover seemed to notice at all.

"So, Emily, about that little *arrangement* of ours," Kent started as we were about ready to finish with the main course.

I perked up at that and Julie did too, slightly, at least looking up and sharing a glance with Kent and Emily.

"Yes, it's hit a bit of a snag," Emily said with a roll of her eyes.

A snag. A business arrangement. That's how she was referring to her daughter.

Somehow, now it was insulting and infuriating. I'd known all along that she had no respect for Lily or even the tiniest bit of emotion in her callous soul for the girl, yet when it wasn't me she was being pandered off to, it was enraging. My grip on the whiskey glass tightened and I took a long swig from it just to keep myself occupied with something other than screaming in her face.

"Are you saying we will not be going through with it?" Kent asked, sneaking a look at me as well before turning his attention back to Emily.

It was obvious that they'd discussed this before, and that he knew full well that Lily belonged to me.

"I'm saying I'll find you something better. This one was... damaged goods."

I stood up so fast that I almost kicked the table over. Emily looked at me sharply, the glare going unnoticed by Kent and Julie as they were trying to right the table before anything fell.

"Whoa there!" Kent chuckled. "You alright there, Lawson?"

Before I could respond, Emily rushed to speak for me.

"He's fine, just a little on the edge, aren't you, Lawson? Maybe you need a little bit of fresh air to clear your mind, before you do something we both regret... like spilling our roast on the table!"

She and Kent were both laughing at her little joke, but I saw the tension in Emily's face. She knew she'd fucked up with her choice of words, but of course the little bitch wasn't going to correct herself.

"Excuse me," I spat out through gritted teeth, grabbing my glass and pulling my smokes out of my pocket before I even made it out of the room.

I had to get a handle on myself, that much was true. I couldn't just fucking go off on Emily now, not when Lily hadn't had much time to put distance between herself and this wretched place she'd once called home. But it was so fucking hard keeping my temper in check around there pretentious fucks who thought the worth of a human life was the price tag they put on it.

I made it out to the balcony off the dining room and lit up immediately, slumping against the wall. It was getting dark outside and I couldn't help but think back to Lily and our bittersweet goodbye last night. I wondered where she was, if she was safe... If I'd done the right thing.

She'd never asked me, so I'd never told her how I got into this, but the situation made me really fucking consider my choices in life. The first job had been because I didn't have enough cash to pay back my bookie, so he referred me to a guy who had 'alternative means' of obtaining income. After the first job, I was hooked, and never looked back.

It didn't take long during that first job to discover I had a knack for breaking people and building them up again. And if there was anything sweeter than giving a woman her first real orgasm, I hadn't seen it yet.

I'd thought myself better than the rest. I was cruel, sure, but I had a method. Rules that could be followed and learned, rewards that came with keeping to those rules. I was strict, but fair, and I thought the women I'd trained and broken had benefitted from that.

It wasn't until far later than I started looking past the immediate gratification and thinking about what happened to them after they left me.

Chloe was the one that broke my spirit, learning what had become of her. No amount of rules and rewards could have saved her from what that fucking maniac did to her. And now, with Lily... a big part of me wished I'd never gotten into this business to begin with.

And another part of me wished I'd never grown a fucking conscience and still had her here with me.

"Sorry," a soft voice said, kicking me out of my thoughts.

Julie slipped through the gap in the sliding door and stepped out on the balcony, closing the door carefully behind her. I frowned, but didn't question her presence. Maybe Emily and Kent were too much for her as well.

"Could I ask for a smoke?"

"Sure," I said, holding the pack out for her and then helping her light it.

Her hands were shaking so hard she could barely hold onto it and she was shivering. It wasn't that cold outside.

"You alright?"

"I will be," she said with an exhale of smoke. "I hope."

Don't we all. It was a sentiment I could definitely understand.

CHAPTER 24

Lily

J MANAGED TO FIND A CAB driving down the lonely
road a mile away from Law's lodge. I'd walked the
mile in my stupid pretty little flats, definitely not
designed for walking, and my feet were covered in blisters.
The ride was expensive too, making me regretfully hand
over too much money. Money I couldn't afford to waste.

But I didn't care about anything other than revenge in
that moment. All I wanted was to make sure my mom got
what was coming to her, and the idea of calling her out
on her shit replayed in my mind a thousand times as we

drove toward our house. Law's truck was parked in the driveway.

I got out of the cab in a hurry, running up the property to the backdoor. I knew my mom liked to keep it open in case she nipped out for a cigarette, which she would never admit to. But it worked in my favor this time—the door was unlocked.

I stared at the house for a little while, all illuminated and pretty from the inside. What a story those walls would tell if they could fucking speak.

And I was going back into that house of horrors, voluntarily.

I pushed open the back door and walked into the kitchen. I heard voices coming from the dining room, strained laughter and polite conversation. Perfect—it meant I'd be able to humiliate mom in front of more people. The bigger audience to watch her go down in flames, the better.

In my mind, it also equated to safety. She couldn't do anything insane if there were people around, right?

I felt self-conscious for a moment, hesitating in the kitchen and wondering if I should really do it. Expose her for the fraud she really was and tell everyone what she was trying to do.

I battled with my inner demons, my mind demanding I shouldn't betray my mom. But in the end, the memory of my dad going down the stairs into the cellar prevailed. I strode into the dining room.

When my mother saw me, she clutched the glass of wine in her hand so tightly the stem snapped.

"A good thing that's white wine," I said coolly. "Otherwise it would be one hell of a stain to get out."

"Lily!" mom hissed. "What are you doing here?"

I looked at everyone in the room. A man and a woman, obviously a couple, were sitting across the table from my mom. The table was set for four people, yet one setting was left untouched. Law. I needed to make sure he was okay.

"Think you'd gotten rid of me?" I asked mom angrily. "Think you could sweep everything under the rug like you've done so many times before?"

She laughed nervously, waving her hand dismissively in my direction.

"Don't mind my daughter," she told her speechless guests. "She's just a little tired."

"Tired, tired of your shit—that's right," I snarled at her.

The man on the other side of the table leered at me.

"Quite the little mouth on her," he said thoughtfully. "Isn't this the one, Emily...?" he asked loosely, giving my mother an inquisitive look.

I chose to ignore his comments and turned to face my mother again.

"I know what you did," I told mom. "I know you killed my dad. I know you're trying to do it again! I know you want to poison Law."

She stared at me coolly, not giving even the smallest reaction. It only made me angrier.

"And," I spat out at her. "I know what you tried to do to me."

I faced her guests. The woman was looking at me with her eyes wide, and the man was drinking me in. Gross.

"She tried to fucking sell her own daughter," I told them. "She tried to sell me to some rich prick as a sex toy."

The woman, who'd looked rattled before, paled and covered her mouth with her hand, but I wasn't done just yet.

"She even fucked the buyer's wife," I told them, looking at my mom for a reaction. "She'd do anything for money. She doesn't give a fuck about me, her husband or the woman she's been sleeping with. All she cares about is getting what she wants."

"That's quite enough, Lily," mom said sternly, standing from her seat, and I glared at her.

This wasn't going quite to plan. I didn't know what I expected would happen, but everyone was being too calm. I wanted reactions, I wanted a big fight. I wanted to end my mother for what she'd done to our family.

I wanted Law.

"I'm going to find him," I told her. "And tell him what you've been trying to do."

The color finally drained from her face and fanned her face, laughing nervously.

"No one is going to believe you, Lily," she said roughly. "You're just a stupid, selfish little girl."

I stepped up to her, looking her right in the eyes.

"Just watch me," I told her. "I'm going to make sure everyone knows who you really are."

As I walked out of the room in search of Law, I felt that man's eyes on me, following my every move. I tried to push it to the back of my mind as I ran up the stairs, crying out for Law. My heart beat with a crazy need to see him, fuck him, tell him things I should've really kept to myself. I felt so confident, I almost got off on the high.

But he was nowhere to be found.

I went through the upper floors of the house, all of the bedrooms. Not a sign of him, or anyone else for that matter.

I ran back down. I'd seen his truck in the driveway, so he had to be somewhere nearby.

As I reached the bottom of the stairs, I bumped into a broad-shouldered, much taller than me figure.

I looked up, and took a step back.

It was the man from the dinner table, the one who'd stared me down and made me feel uncomfortable. I hadn't realized how fucking tall he was when he was sitting down, but he was definitely towering over me now.

"W-what do you want?" I asked, hating myself for stuttering.

"You," he replied, flashing me a devilish grin.

I looked around us to find a way to escape. I didn't like this man. He made me feel deeply uncomfortable. There was just something off about him. Any normal person would have balked at my statements at the dinner table, but he didn't seem to care much at all.

The realization hit me too late.

"Please move," I asked and tried to get past him, but he wouldn't let me.

His enormous, meaty hand wrapped around my forearm and stopped me in my tracks. I looked up into his dark, threatening eyes. My heart was beating out of order, every beat accompanied by panic being shot through my veins.

"Not so fast, little bird," he told me with a grin. "I want to get a good look at you."

"Why?" I asked.

He gave me a meaningful look and that was when it finally sunk in.

"You're the buyer," I said breathlessly.

"Ding ding ding! Bingo," he mocked me, a grin spreading over his face.

He was a very handsome man. Not so much unlike Law—tall, dark and handsome, except his eyes were a murky brown where Law's were gray. But he made me feel scared, really, really scared. Not in the way Law did, where excitement took precedence. This man made me want to run as fast as I could in the other direction, when Law had always made me want to run to him.

"I'm not for fucking sale," I bit out, and his fingers dug into my arm.

"Language," he reminded me roughly, then chuckled. "Your mom painted you as a sweet, naive little virgin, Lily. Another lie, I presume."

"I'm not a virgin," I told him pointedly, hoping that would dissuade him from pursuing this sale.

"Ah." His eyes sparkled with mischief. "Lawson?"

I glared at him and he laughed again.

I moved to get away, and he yanked me back. I cried out, the pain of him pulling on my arm so intense my eyes watered.

"You're hurting me," I said softly.

"It's just the beginning, dear," he said with a smile. "Just the beginning of what I'm going to do to you."

I swallowed a sob and tried to hit him where it hurt.

"My mom's sleeping with your wife," I reminded him. "Maybe you should focus on that."

"I don't give a shit," he told me roughly. "Julie's a spineless frigid bitch. Maybe that's why they like each other—your mom has balls of steel... for a frigid bitch, anyway."

His own joke made him laugh and I tried to use the distraction to get away from him again. I pulled, but instead of letting go, he yanked me closer until my back was flush against his chest. He caged me in, his hand curling around my neck and cutting off my air supply.

"Not so fast, little bird," he groaned.

I cried out. He was hard, I could feel his erection.

"Get the fuck off her."

I followed the sound of the voice. Law was standing in the doorway, the patio doors leading outside. A half-smoked cigarette smoldered in his hand. He dropped it to the ground and stomped on it. His expression was unreadable, dark and dangerous like the first few times in the cellar.

"Come to stake your claim?" the buyer mocked him. "You really brainwashed this one, Lawson."

He let go of me and pushed me forward until I stumbled into Law's arms. He embraced me roughly and I clung to him.

"Guess hot pussy runs in the family," the buyer laughed. "Like mother, like daughter."

I felt Law tense, but it was me who stepped forward and smacked the man in the face, hard.

He didn't budge, but it felt so fucking good to see the rage on his face, to know I'd actually stood up for myself.

"Do not fucking ever compare me to her," I hissed at him.

He merely grinned, soothing his bright red cheek.

"Get lost," Law told him.

"You gonna let a girl do your dirty work, Lawson?" the buyer mocked him.

Law pulled me aside and stepped forward. He made a single move, a loud crack echoing in the room followed by the buyer's scream.

The man's right arm was hanging crookedly and uselessly next to his body.

"Fucker," he snarled at Law, cradling his broken arm.

"Get. Lost. Now." Law punctuated every word by breaking his fingers. "Three down. Do I need to break them all?"

I felt myself getting sick from the disgusting crunchy sound of bones breaking.

The buyer stumbled back, glaring at us.

"Fucked up family," he muttered under his breath. And then he was finally gone.

Law's shoulders tensed once we were alone and I tried to control my erratic breaths as his posture fell. Would he be mad that I'd come to the house? Had I done the right thing?

"What are you doing here, Lily?" he asked me sternly, turning around to face me.

"I had to come," I cried out. "You're in danger, Law."

"What?"

"My mom," I told him. "I... I think she's poisoning you. Or planning to poison you."

He gave me a blank stare.

"She did it to my dad." My voice was shaky. "I... I remembered. When you left. She's done this before. She'd never let you disobey her."

"Lily."

He stepped closer to me and I ran into his arms.

"I know," I said. "You told me not to come. But I had to. You can punish me all you want, but..."

I looked into his eyes. They were brighter than ever.

"I'm not leaving, Law. You can't make me. We can take her. We can fight."

There was a war going on inside of him.

"This is the fucking last time," he growled. "That you call me by my name to my face."

I grinned.

"Is that fucking clear, babygirl?"

"Yes," I couldn't help but smile.

"Yes?" he taunted me.

"Yes, Daddy."

He claimed my lips, a deep kiss that left my mouth feeling hot and needy. He pushed his tongue between my lips, demanding that I submit to him. And this time, I did it freely. I wanted to be his babygirl forever.

"Don't send me away again," I begged him against his mouth, and he bit my bottom lip, making me cry out.

"You're not getting rid of me," he promised me. "Daddy's gonna keep you, Lily."

My heart soared when I heard those words coming from his lips. No matter what happened next, I would always have this moment.

When the beast fell for the brat, making her grow up in the process.

CHAPTER 25

Law

I'D NEVER FELT A HIGH like the one I was experiencing with Lily back in my arms. Letting her go had been the worst mistake I'd ever made, even if at the time, it felt like the only thing I could do.

I hadn't banked on her being this brave... or maybe this stupid, but if that was the case then you could say the same for both of us. I was more than happy to be in the same fucking boat with her.

I kissed her forehead when I'd claimed the breath from her lungs and crushed her against my chest, completely forgetting that we were still in the same house with Emily and Julie. Kent was a distant afterthought. I might have made a powerful enemy that night, but I sure as fuck wasn't going to spare him a single bit of my attention for the rest of the evening.

I could stand there forever, just kissing and holding my babygirl, completely ignoring the tough choices we would have to make next. A sharp, shocked scream was what shook me from my reverie, snapping my attention back into the moment. Back to the danger we were both in, sharing a house with Emily.

I'd have to ask Lily exactly what she meant by what she'd told me, but I didn't need any additional confirmation to know that Emily was dangerous. More so to Lily than she was to me.

"Come on," I told her, releasing her from my grip but grabbing her hand tightly in mine.

I didn't want to let her go again, not for a second.

"That sounded like my mother," she said softly, her brows knitting together as I tugged her forward.

We rushed through the house toward where the noise had come from. There was more commotion in the kitchen, so I guided us there. The moment I stepped through the door, I knew I shouldn't have brought Lily here.

"Shit," I muttered, grabbing her and making her turn her back to the kitchen, holding her head against my chest. "You don't need to see this, Lily."

"What?! Let me see!" she gasped, probably catching the tone of my voice and knowing something bad was going on.

She struggled against me just as Emily groaned, blood bubbling out of her mouth as she lay on her perfectly tiled kitchen floor, bleeding out of her abdomen. Julie was standing over her, her face a mask of shock and rage all at once, holding the same damn knife we'd used to carve the roast.

"Julie, put that down," I said, keeping my voice level.

"Please let me see," Lily almost hissed at me, panic high in her voice.

Reluctantly, I let her go. I might need my hands to get that knife away from Julie and as much as I would have preferred to protect Lily from this moment altogether, I knew that I couldn't shield her from everything.

She spun around, freezing in spot as her gaze hit her mother.

Emily, so put together and always flawless, was sprawled out, the delicate gown she'd chosen for the evening ripped in several places. I could count multiple puncture wounds, but it was the deep gash across her abdomen that was going to be the end of her. Through the thick, crimson blood, I could see broken intestines, which Emily was desperately trying to shove back within her stomach cavity.

"Mom," Lily whispered, covering her mouth with her hand a moment later.

Emily's face was drained of color and I could see the flicker going out of her eyes. She was moments from dying and I knew there was nothing I could do about it, even if I'd wanted to.

"Lily, call the ambulance," I said. "Lily, now."

That's what snapped her into motion. She turned and ran out of the kitchen, doing as she was told. I knew I had to take control of this situation, because apparently I was the only fucking adult in the building.

"Julie, put the knife down. Don't make me tell you again."

I moved closer slowly. Julie kept her grip on the knife, looking down at Emily, her face an unreadable mask of indifference. Gone was the shaky little woman I'd shared a cigarette with outside. This was a warrior, out on a mission. I wondered how I'd missed it before.

"Not yet," she said calmly, holding a hand up to me. "Give me a moment."

"Where's Kent?"

"Crying somewhere about his arm," Julie said with a shrug. "He deserved it, though."

I couldn't agree with her more.

Emily couldn't utter a word. In another couple of seconds, I saw the last flashes of surprise and pain seep out of her gaze, and all that was left was the cold depths of her blue eyes, staring lifelessly at the ceiling. Julie let out a breath and with a small smile, she put down the knife on the kitchen counter, as if she was only now satisfied that she wouldn't need it anymore.

"I knew," she said, slumping against the counter with one hip, staring down at Emily. "Because of Kent... I knew what she was doing. I ignored it for years... I ignored what Kent did for years. But this, this was too much. The people she was selling... they were children, practically.

"She thought she was getting close to Kent through me, but it was the other way around. I didn't think I'd actually go through with it. I didn't think I would... I can't believe that I did!"

She looked at me with bright eyes and a smile warmer than any I'd seen on her. Instinctively, I reached into my back pocket and offered her the pack of cigarettes. Julie giggled as she snatched one of them out and I helped her light it.

"Some dinner," I said, not joining her in having a smoke.

I didn't need one anymore. I had Lily now, that was all the addiction I was capable of handling.

"It'll go down in history," Julie chuckled, proudly looking down at her handiwork, the pool of blood around Emily's body slowly spreading across the tiles.

It was almost up to Julie's peeptoed shoes.

"You know I'm going to have to call the cops now, right?" I asked her.

"I know," she said with a nod. "But it was worth it."

My only regret was that I hadn't done it before Julie had to.

CHAPTER 26

Lily

Three months later

"DO YOU LIKE IT, BABYGIRL?"

I twirled around the spacious living room area, not caring if my skirt riding up revealed my butt. I smiled wide at Law and clapped my hands excitedly, jumping up and down at the mere idea of it.

"Yes!" I told him. "I love it. I love it so much. It's absolutely perfect."

This was the tenth house we'd come to see. And it was the first one that felt like home to me. I knew we'd found the right place the moment we stopped in front of the building and I got a look at the big, spacious yard, perfect for having kids and a dog running around and playing.

It had only been three months since my mother's death, but it felt like I'd lived a lifetime since then. Probably because I never felt like I'd lived much at all with her shadow still over me.

I was back in school, working on my degree—though I'd switched my major to social work now—and there hadn't been a day I hadn't spent with Law and loved every second of it. He was just as rough and brutal and unpredictable as ever, but also kind, loving and fiercely protective of me.

Julie was awaiting trial for my mother's murder, though I couldn't harbor any hate for her in my heart. She'd done the right thing, as fucked up as it was. Kent had been brought up on charges for human trafficking, based on Julie's testimony. I hoped it would let her get a lighter sentence.

As shocking as it was to realize that my mother was dead, I couldn't help but think that the world was a better place for it. I was determined to spend my life exposing others like her and the people Law had once worked for in the name of sparing innocent people.

I mean, I would be the last person to claim that I was impartial about all of this, but I knew right from wrong. There was a difference between giving yourself into a situation like the one Law and I now had—though it hadn't begun that way—and being forced into it.

Law turned to face the wide-eyed realtor, who tried to keep the judgment off her expression. I gave her a questioning look and her face was wiped clean of emotion in the next moment. Good. She'd get paid a hefty commission for this sale.

"We'll take it," Law told her, and she beamed.

"Excellent," she nodded, scribbling something down in her notebook, which was already overflowing with papers and notes. "I'll contact the sellers and we should sort out the initial deposit in the next few weeks..."

"No," Law interrupted her, his hand in the air and motioning for her to stop. "We're buying the house. Now."

"But I..."

The realtor looked frazzled as hell.

"Cash," Law told her. "Or I can wire the money into the company's account now, and we can sign the papers as soon as possible. I want the keys now, though."

The realtor opened and closed her mouth like a fish out of water, finally squeaking out a reply.

"Let me make a quick phone call."

She excused herself and made her way outside while Law joined me in the bare living room. I loved that the house was new. No bad history to follow us, just a fresh start—exactly what we needed.

Law would get to do some work with his hands, make some improvements to the house and maybe even build some furniture. I could busy myself with decorating, making sure everything look as perfect as I imagined in my head.

I wanted our home to be a place we both loved, a place where we both felt safe.

"You really love it, babygirl?" Law asked me, pulling me into his arms.

"Yes!" I nodded eagerly. "I love it. I feel safe here."

"Then that's all that matters." Law's voice was gentle as he kissed me, but the kiss was far from innocent.

The realtor walked back in in the middle of it and cleared her throat awkwardly to get out attention. Law gave her a look that said 'fuck off' in no uncertain terms.

"They, er, they agreed," she said, and I yelped with delight.

Half an hour later, and we held the signed papers in our hands. After Law had offered twenty grand above the asking price, the previous owner came over along with some officials to sign the contract. And then we were officially homeowners.

A real home, not some pretense for one like the house I grew up in.

When Law shut the door after they left, I let out a long breath. He glanced at me before advancing on me like I was prey and he was the predator. I would never get sick of the way this man looked at me.

"Daddy, please." I slipped into my role so easily, it made him groan out loud.

Law hated it when we had company, when I called him anything but Daddy. He reached me in a few long steps, lifting me up and making me giggle as his hands found their way under my skirt, greedy fingers pulling my panties down my ass.

He walked us back until we reached the kitchen counter, one of the only finished things in the house. He put me down and I wrapped my legs around his waist tightly, leaning my body back slightly from him to tease him.

"I thought they'd never fucking leave," he groaned. "I've been so fucking hard for you since you twirled around in that slutty little skirt of yours, babygirl."

It was a constant challenge in my mind, trying to keep

him hard and ready to ravage me as often as I possibly could.

I was giggling as he reached for my blouse and gasped when he ripped it open in a single motion.

"Daddy!" I pouted. "That was new!"

"I'll buy you a new one," he muttered against my neck. "Anything my babygirl wants. Now fucking strip for Daddy before I lose it."

He helped me wriggle out of my skirt and I moaned out loud when I felt his hardness press up against my tummy as he held me close.

"I'm going to fuck you on every surface of this house," Law promised me. "Every fucking room."

"Yes, Daddy. Please..."

I bit his neck gently as he pulled my panties aside, exposing my raw pink slit. I was wet already, my pussy so needy for his cock it was as if we hadn't even fucked in the car on the way over. Law had pulled over and taken me over the hood of the car, not giving a shit if anyone saw. I came so hard my voice was still raspy from screaming his name.

"What does my babygirl want?" he grunted against my ear, and I squirmed under his hands.

"I want Daddy," I breathed. "I want Daddy in my pussy."

"Yes, babygirl. Whatever you want."

I unzipped him and he pulled out his cock, big and throbbing, the tip slick with precum. It never ceased to amaze me how big he was, and how he'd stretched my pussy to fit the shape of his cock perfectly.

"I want this to be special, babygirl," he told me, and my eyes left his cock, glazing over.

"How, Daddy?"

He took ahold of my hair, grabbing it at the nape of my neck and making me mewl as he pulled on it, hard.

"Daddy's gonna breed you, babygirl," he whispered in the shell of my ear, and I squirmed under his needy fingers. "Daddy's gonna put a baby in your belly tonight."

"Fuck," I breathed, trying not to gasp as I took deep gulps of air.

"Don't curse. Good girls don't curse," he said, grabbing my ass so hard it hurt a little. "Do you want that?" His voice was gentle as he teased my entrance with the tip of his cock. "Do you want Daddy to breed you, Lily?"

"Yes," I begged. "Daddy please! I want you..."

"What do you want, babygirl?" he asked, his hazy eyes looking into mine.

I smiled mischievously, thinking of the perfect answer.

"I want Daddy's little monster," I giggled. "Growing in his babygirl's belly."

With a loud groan, Law pushed himself inside me,

filling me up and bottoming out in my pussy. I cried out as he fucked me, deep, raw thrusts that shook me to my core. He took what he wanted, just like he'd taken me the first time, along with my virginity.

Once I came from his deep thrusts I couldn't stop myself. I cried out for him again and again and it only made him fuck me harder.

"Fuck a baby into me, Daddy," I moaned in his ear, and with a groan, he unloaded inside me.

I mewled as I came again, my whole body shaking. Law pulled out his still throbbing cock and I complained weakly as he grabbed my legs and tipped me back so I was lying down.

"Legs up," he grinned at me. "Make sure it runs deep inside you, babygirl."

I stared at him with dreamy eyes as I came down from my high.

"I love you, Daddy," I whispered.

Law grinned at me and held my legs up, running a finger over my pussy and making me twitch.

"Daddy loves you too, babygirl," he told me. "You're my special little girl. And Daddy wants to make you his completely."

I thought of his seed running down inside me and grinned at him.

"Are we fucked up, Daddy?" I asked him with a wicked grin, and he laughed out loud.

"The most fucked up, babygirl," he promised, smacking my ass hard.

EPILOGUE

Law

Two years later.

*L*ILY WAS SITTING ON MY lap, her eyes transfixed on the stage. Amber, one-half of a duo we had come to think of as regulars, was writhing on the stage, held up by chains linking around her wrists as Jonathan whipped her back. Every smack that hit her bare skin sent her body propelling forward, only to be stopped by the restraints.

Pleasure and pain mixed on Amber's face, the blindfold covering her eyes but her lips parted in a scream that waxed and waned. When the lashes didn't come fast enough, she'd beg loudly, practically screeching for him to keep going.

And Lily was eating it up, as she always did.

My hand was between her legs, my fingers rubbing her sweet wet pussy and parting it slowly, but not pressing in quite yet. She'd keep squirming a little, but every time she did, I'd pull my fingers back, reminding her to behave or she wouldn't get what she wanted so badly.

When she kept still, I'd press my fingers forward again, gliding over her clit and then starting to penetrate her. A small moan escaped her lips and my cock throbbed painfully in my pants, begging to be let out and fed to my babygirl.

As Jonathan threw aside the whip and unzipped, I pushed my fingers inside of Lily, two at the same time. She tensed, her back going rigid for a moment, before easing into it. I loved the satisfied sigh that crossed her lips, making me bite the inside of my mouth.

I didn't have any attention to spare for Jonathan and Amber, all I could focus on was the way my babygirl was begging for my fingers to be in her pussy. So I obliged.

I pushed them in deeper, until my knuckles were pressed against her cunt, and then pulled out only to do it all over again. As Jonathan started fucking Amber right there on the stage, in front of dozens of hungry eyes, I was fingerfucking Lily on the best seat in the house.

She leaned back a little, propping her hands on my thighs so she wouldn't topple over. She ground against my hand and I allowed it now, she'd behaved so well. When Jonathan picked up rhythm, obvious by the way Amber was screaming, so did I, slamming into Lily harder.

She fell back, her head on my shoulder, and my free hand went to her tits. I groped them through the shirt she was wearing, no bra under it just like I'd asked. She'd gotten a little curvier since the pregnancy and I loved it just as much as I'd loved her slimmer physique. Her curves were fucking heavenly.

"Daddy," she gasped, whispering in my ear. "Please, more!"

I shoved her legs wide open and started fucking her harder with my fingers, knowing full well that no one cared or would look at us in our own damn club. She was moaning and writhing in my lap, her squeals rising to a crescendo in time with Amber.

When she squirted all over my hand, I chuckled, kissing her neck roughly.

"Good girl," I told her, keeping my fingers inside of her and moving them slowly now, keeping her on that edge of being overstimulated but wanting more and more.

"Anything for you," she purred, kissing my cheek.

I pulled out of her finally and smoothed the pink thong she'd worn as I'd told her to back over her shaved pussy. She righted herself on my lap and then stood up. I was still hard as a rock.

"Is there anything I can do for you, Daddy?" she asked mischievously, that spark in her eye that I'd grown so used to.

There hadn't been a day since we got out of that house of horrors when I hadn't seen that twinkle in her eyes at least for a while. There were harder times and easier times, but we always persevered, and the joy we felt had only grown since our son, Thomas, was born.

It had been a while since we'd been in the club, taking time after the pregnancy to get settled in our own rhythm. But I'd started building it up not long after we bought the house, knowing that there had to be a healthy way for people like Lily and I to indulge our darker side.

We'd created a safe place for people with the same kind of dark tastes, a club where everyone with good intentions were welcome and the only thing that could be done to you was what you asked for. If you asked to not be given a choice... well, then that was exactly what you got.

"Soon," I told Lily, standing up reluctantly and roping my arm around her waist. "I want to show you off before."

She smiled at me, slipping her hand in my back pocket.

"Are you showing off your wifey or your little girl?" she asked.

"Both," I told her, and I meant it.

There was separation between our fantasies and our reality, especially with Thomas in the picture now, but deep down inside, the connection we had formed transcended the fantasy. I was always going to look after her, I was always going to fight for her and protect her like a Daddy had to, regardless of what we called it.

She would always be my little girl, no matter how grown up she was and what kind of day-to-day crap we had to deal with.

And I was always going to be hers, because the two of us, well... we completed one another. I'd been a monster when she found me, and I probably always would be... but I was her monster now. That was never going to change.

Made in the
USA
Middletown, DE